# THE HINDERWOOD

## JAKE NICKENS

For Julia and Christian

# TABLE OF CONTENTS

# PRELUDE

William Porter woke from a dreamless sleep. When he woke, he did not sit up, or roll over, or even open his eyes—he lay still, and he listened carefully.

For a few moments, he heard nothing…

Then, the soft noise that disrupted his sleep sounded again. With a sigh, William Porter rose from his mattress and walked to the door of his bedroom.

As he passed the edge of his bed, a massive form stirred in the darkness. The enormous shadow—whose blackness stood out even in the dark room—expressed a sleepy and mildly irritated question to William Porter.

"Let's go see, girl."

The shadow rose dutifully and followed him out of the room. Together, they cautiously descended a wooden staircase to the main level of the old building.

A network of coffins rested on ornate pedestals, but William Porter didn't need any light to navigate through them. He moved with purpose, heading straight to a metal door that read, "Employees Only."

He pushed on the heavy door and held it open for the large creature to pass through ahead of him. Then,

William Porter followed, unbothered by the smell of chemicals and cleaning supplies that filled the air. The tile floor felt cold on his bare feet, and he took special care to step over the metal drain in the middle of the room, making his way to a small door on the other side. A faint red glow settled briefly on William and his large companion as they stepped into the night, cast down from the "Exit" sign overhead.

Walking across cool, wet grass, the two figures kept all eyes on a structure about a hundred yards out from the main building. A pale, flickering lightbulb hung near the front of the small shack, helping William to see clearly—though he did not need that help. He knew every square inch of the shed's exterior better than he knew the lines on his own weathered face.

An iron bar barricaded the two wooden doors, and a chain ran between the handles, held securely in place by a heavy padlock. If anyone looked closely enough, they might just make out strange symbols etched into both the lock and the chain.

William looked closely. Nothing seemed out of order with any of the security measures, causing the mortician to sigh with relief. Those doors had remained sealed tight for almost a hundred years, but he still got antsy when any errant noise caught his attention. He turned to the dark shape beside him.

"Must be getting old," he said, smiling wryly at his own bad joke. Then, he turned and took two steps back toward the building.

*Thump*! … *Thump*!

William Porter whirled around. Nothing changed about the lock, or the chains, or the iron bar, but, as he stared at the door, there was a slight shudder, and—

*Thump!* … *Thump!*

A knock came from inside the shed.

His companion growled, and the darkness peeled back to reveal a flash of white: a massive set of teeth baring at the double doors. William sighed again, but this time with resignation. He walked around to the other side of the small building and returned with a metal folding chair, which he opened in one motion and placed near the shed doors. He took a seat, then motioned for his companion to do the same.

"Get comfortable," he said. "I think we're in for a long night."

# CHAPTER ONE

Jimmy knew he messed up when he heard bike tires spinning through loose gravel behind him. Then, he realized the depth of his mistake when he saw that the fences on either side of him were too high to climb quickly.

He didn't panic; his brother always said that panicking turned an already-tough situation stupid. Jimmy thought it wasn't exactly the kind of thing to put on a motivational poster, but, like most things his brother said, it had a kind of blunt, reassuring truth to it. So, Jimmy didn't waste time panicking; instead, he quickly scanned the fenced lane ahead of him—and he bolted, in the opposite direction from the bikes.

Jimmy was fast, perhaps too fast for a twelve-year-old. Earlier that day, he was called into Principal Folk's office who, along with an excited Coach Throckmorton, informed him that his four-hundred-yard sprint time was so good, he was being given a starting spot on the relay team. The relay team traditionally consisted of eighth graders, and Jimmy had never heard of a sixth grader making the team.

He didn't share the coach's excitement, though. After all, Jimmy wasn't just fast; he was smart, too. He was the youngest in his grade, because the school advanced him early due to academic achievement.

So, Jimmy knew immediately that if the coach put him on the relay team, someone else had been cut.

"There he is!" Jimmy heard the shout behind him as the sound of the bikes drew closer.

He didn't look back; he kept his breath steady and ran faster, nearing the end of the fenced alley. If he could make it out, if he could get off the gravel path and into the woods, he knew the trees were too thick for his pursuers to follow on bike. And they'd be no match for him on foot.

Suddenly, another bike shot out in front of him. Jimmy flinched and tried to spin around the obstacle, but the bike kept moving and boxed him in. He looked up at the rider, hoping it was some random adult in spandex shorts. But Keegan Hill grinned down at him.

Jimmy's breath caught in his throat.

"Where you going, Jim?"

"...Just heading home."

"You mean that crazy old lady's shack?" Keegan taunted. "That'll have to wait." He picked at something in his teeth and continued, "Miles wants to talk to you."

Keegan swung a big leg over his bike and let it fall to the ground. Jimmy looked up at him. Keegan was a farm kid. He wasn't much taller than Jimmy, and he was overweight, but he had quick hands and a toughness that made him a formidable nose guard for the JV football team. Jimmy knew it would be hard to get around him, but not impossible, as long as the others didn't—

"You in a hurry, Doe?"

Jimmy groaned internally but tried not to look frightened. Instinctively, he brushed the rabbit's foot key chain in his pocket, like he always did when he felt nervous. His brother gave him the key chain to calm him when he was little, and brushing it became a kind of tic over the years.

He turned around and saw Miles Crawford and the Davis twins getting off their bikes. He was surrounded.

Jimmy tried to remain calm. He forced himself to smile nonchalantly at Miles as the older boy stepped closer.

Miles Crawford was the meanest kid at Opossum Trot Public Middle School. He was in the seventh grade, but he'd been held back twice, so the older boy towered over all the other students. He had a shaved head and a lean, wiry physique. Looking at Miles, he seemed like a natural fit for track. But he just didn't have the speed—not like Jimmy—so, Coach cut him to make room for the new recruit.

"What's up, Miles?" Jimmy asked, his eyes dropping to Miles's right hand. It held a hammer.

"Wanted to ask you something, if you aren't in a hurry?" Miles grinned, displaying teeth badly in need of orthodontic attention.

"I just promised Ms. Dubois I'd help her with some things. I'll have to catch up with y'all later."

13

Jimmy turned to step casually around Keegan, but the larger boy chuckled maliciously and moved to block his path.

Over his shoulder, Jimmy heard Miles say, "We were just wondering how you were going to do the relay team with a broken foot."

As he realized Miles was serious, Jimmy's back stiffened, momentarily paralyzed by fear. But he forced down the feeling of panic rising in his belly and surveyed his captors. They were all bigger. But he would have to lash out at one of them and, hopefully, create enough of a distraction to run for it.

"Yeah, y'all are scary," said another, drier voice.

Jimmy turned around when he heard him. So did Miles and the Davis twins. He couldn't see Miles's face, but Jimmy could guess his expression. After all, though Miles was the *meanest* kid in Opossum Trot Public Middle School, he definitely wasn't the *scariest* kid in town.

No, Jimmy and every other kid at school knew that particular honor went to Jimmy's older brother Jack.

Jack Doe stood a couple yards away from the other boys. Jimmy had no idea how he'd gotten so close without anyone hearing him, but Jack always was a mystery. As Jimmy might have expected, Jack had the Heaven Breaker with him.

All the other boys' gazes fixed on it.

The "Heaven Breaker" was Jack Doe's baseball bat. When he first decided to play baseball, Jack got the notion from Buford and Cash of making a bat by hand.

Jimmy listened with Jack to the two crazy old veterans rambling on about samurais forging their own swords, and he knew his brother was sold on the idea. Jack dragged Jimmy on a ten-mile hike deep into the Nebelwood Forest to find an ash tree suitable for the project. He remembered watching in awe as Jack climbed the tall tree to remove a branch big enough to form the bat.

Jack then spent days shaping and sanding the wood until finally, with a coat of black paint and some leather cord wrapped around the handle, the Heaven Breaker was born. Ever since its creation, Jack had pulverized dozens of baseballs with the hand-carved bat. When he could be bothered to show up for games, the sight of Jack stepping up to the plate with his weapon of choice was enough to dishearten the most formidable of JV pitchers.

Now, Jack held the bat loosely at his side and stared at Miles with unnerving calm.

"This whole thing, with the bikes—" Jack nodded at the high fence surrounding them. "—and the alley. Very intimidating. Who came up with it? I doubt it was Keegan."

Keegan sneered at Jack, but with less bravado than before, and pushed past Jimmy.

Looking around, Jimmy realized he was on the other side of the bullies. He could have escaped easily if he wished.

But after a glance at Jack, he decided to stick around and see how things unfolded.

15

Jack took a step closer to Miles, who glared down at Jack. They were both fifteen, but Miles had a couple inches on the eldest Doe brother. Jack didn't seem to mind. Jimmy noticed Miles tighten his grip on the hammer, though.

"Just 'cause you're crazy don't mean I'm scared of you, Doe," Miles sneered.

Jack's arm blurred, and he slammed his bat into Miles's hand.

Jimmy, Keegan, and the Davis twins all winced as the hammer flew into the gravel.

Miles groaned, then the color drained from his face. He doubled over, cupping his hand gingerly.

Jack's face was expressionless, his voice soft as he whispered, "You sure?"

Miles swung his undamaged hand in a wild haymaker at Jack, who ducked and shoved him to the ground with the momentum.

Keegan made an angry grunting sound and charged toward Jack. Jimmy thought this was very unwise, since his brother was still holding the bat and clearly didn't mind using it.

Jack sidestepped the oncoming boy and drove a knee into his stomach. When Keegan doubled over, Jack brought the handle of the bat down on his back, dropping the farm boy into the gravel.

Then, Jack turned toward the Davis twins—but the brothers were already riding away from the violent scene.

He exhaled softly and turned to Jimmy. "Stupid to go home this way."

"I thought I had time to get ahead of them," said Jimmy. "I didn't think they'd be on bikes."

"Should have just waited."

"Well, I kinda wanted to avoid someone getting hurt." Jimmy gestured to the two boys on the ground.

Keegan hunched over, holding his stomach with one hand and supporting himself with the other. Miles labored to try and get to his feet.

"Oh, and Keegan called Ms. Dubois crazy," Jimmy offered.

Jack's foot shot out, knocking Keegan's support arm aside and sending the big boy back into the gravel.

"Yeah, that's real tough of you, getting your brother to fight your fights," said Miles, finally rising to his feet. His right hand swelled red and struggled to close, but it didn't look broken. The other was balled into a fist.

"I don't think you understand," Jack said softly. Both Jimmy and Miles looked at him.

When Jack didn't say anything else, Miles spat, "What?"

"I'm not here to fight for him. A brother evens the odds."

Miles stared, uncomprehending. Jimmy only sighed.

"You have a problem with my brother?" said Jack. "Y'all work it out."

"What?" said Jimmy, complaining but unsurprised.

"What?" echoed Miles, bewildered.

Jack leaned his bat against the alley wall and sat down beside it on the ground. "I just wanted to make it a fair fight."

"You're serious," said Jimmy, shaking his head— not in disbelief, but with a familiar feeling of irritation.

"How is it a fair fight? You screwed up my hand," Miles said with a pout.

"Yeah, but you're older. And you have a reach advantage," said Jack, patiently.

Miles looked at Jimmy, who shrugged. Miles turned back to Jack. "You won't jump in?"

"Nope. Not as long as it's just you."

Miles looked over at Keegan, who sat up but made no move to stand. Then, the older boy chuckled, turning toward Jimmy with a mocking smile. "Alright. Sure, why not? I don't need help with some pansy runt." He took a step toward Jimmy.

Jimmy shot his brother an irritated look.

Jack just nodded encouragingly.

Miles was almost within arm's reach. So, Jimmy sighed and stepped up.

$$\Delta$$

Jimmy winced slightly as he walked home with Jack, touching light fingers to the faint black eye developing on the left side of his face. He sighed, trying to

18

take comfort in knowing Miles had one fewer tooth than he had that morning.

Jack patted him on the back. "I thought you did alright."

"Well, that's great, Jack."

"It's just... you're a lot shorter than him. Seems like you could have ducked that hook."

"I didn't think he'd use that hand."

"Seems like it'd be easy to dodge a messed-up hand."

"We should have just left," said Jimmy, angrily. "They would have let us leave."

"Then you would've had to deal with it some other time. At least it's done."

"Done? You think me and Miles are going to be buds now?"

"No, but I think he's done trying to fight you."

Jimmy just shook his head, familiar with the futility of arguing with Jack about anything.

"What am I going to tell Ms. Dubois? She's going to be pissed about this." Jimmy pointed at the developing black eye.

"Stop at the store and get some foundation or something to cover it up. No sense in upsetting her."

"So, I get a black eye, and now I've got to buy makeup? You want me to tell the cashier I tripped, too?"

Jack shrugged. "Or you got hit by a baseball."

"That was a joke."

"Funny stuff," said Jack, with a deadpan expression.

"You going to Buford and Cash's?" Jimmy asked.

"Just for a couple hours. Still working on the coyote problem."

"Well, try to keep it quick. Everyone's meeting in town before the Challenge."

"I'll meet you at home before it's time to go."

"Cool."

"Cool."

"Guess I'm gonna go buy makeup now."

"Life takes some funny turns."

# CHAPTER TWO

Jack held the rifle steady and stared through the lens of the scope. Fifty yards from the tree-line, the stuffed rabbit he'd won from the crane game at Zo's Pizzeria sat on the ground. Without looking away from it, Jack kept the gun steady on the rest with one hand and tapped a button on his phone with the other.

The small speaker next to the stuffed animal suddenly emitted a noise like a young rabbit in distress. While the crying noises continued, Jack waited.

After a few minutes, Jack noticed a stirring on the edge of the forest. As he watched, two coyotes emerged from the woods, walking low and smoothly toward the stuffed animal. When they got closer, they split up, each approaching from a different side.

Jack shifted the rifle until its crosshairs framed the front shoulder of the coyote closest to the rabbit. His finger moved toward the trigger, but then, some faint movement disturbed his peripheral vision. When he swiveled the rifle slightly, he saw a third coyote emerge from the woods.

Assessing the positioning of all three predators, Jack moved his crosshairs onto the coyote closest to the tree-line. He took a deep but steady breath. Then, he pulled the trigger.

The shot drowned out the rabbit's electronic distress call, and the other coyotes turned their heads in his direction.

But even as the first coyote dropped, Jack ejected the spent shell casing, racked in another load, and shot the coyote to the right of the rabbit. The remaining predator bolted toward the forest, but Jack ejected the second casing, reloaded, and moved the crosshairs. After leading the shot slightly, he pulled the trigger a third time, and a red flash of blood hit a nearby oak. The final coyote's body tumbled to a stop.

After clicking on its safety, Jack leaned the gun against the painted plywood wall of the shooting house. He rubbed his eyes, tired from focusing for so long, and stretched his back. After a brief survey of the cramped space, he got to his feet. The shooting house wobbled slightly when he rose, but the shifting structure did not bother Jack. The makeshift blind was built cheaply, not poorly.

He slung the rifle over his shoulder, opened the door to the box stand, and began climbing down the ladder attached to the tall wooden legs.

When Jack arrived at the first of the bodies, he noticed the coyotes showed early signs of mange, and the skin disease gave the wild dogs an almost zombie-like appearance. The first coyote's ear bent sharply to the right, and its left eye socket was empty. For a moment, Jack wondered if the bullet exited through that eye, but on closer examination, the wound looked much older.

Jack sighed and stood up straight. A flash of red caught his eye, and he instinctively rolled the rifle off his shoulder and into a ready position facing the woods.

At the edge of the trees, a red fox stood staring at Jack. The animal watched him calmly, unconcerned with the nearby corpses or with the rifle pointed in its direction.

Jack kept the rifle steady for a moment, then exhaled and lowered the gun. Foxes posed a danger to Buford and Cash's chickens, but they only hired him to cull the coyotes. As he slung the gun over his shoulder again, he watched the fox. It watched back, unmoving, before eventually trotting into the darkness of the trees.

When the red fur vanished, Jack turned his attention back to the matter at hand. Closing his eyes, he said a prayer for the three predators. That finished, he kept his eyes closed for a moment and felt the quiet of the sunset settle on the scene.

Then, he opened his eyes, and he went to get a shovel to bury the coyotes.

$$\Delta$$

Jack never prayed before meeting Ms. Dubois. He wasn't sure if he believed in God or not, but shortly after they met, he promised her that he would say his prayers every day, regardless. She told him if he prayed every day, especially when he felt lonely or troubled, he would feel more peace in his life. He was absolutely shocked to find that she was correct.

He wasn't sure whether the feeling of focused calm and tranquility came from The Divine or just from the comfort of a ritual, but it was hard to argue with the results, either way. Jack had read enough to know he was a deeply troubled kid, and he would take what he could get.

After his work, he approached the wraparound front porch where Buford and Cash sat together on folding chairs.

"Heard three shots, must be three fewer coyotes getting after the goats and chickens," said Cash. The old Black man nodded approvingly, his camouflage jacket rustling while his *Reagan/Bush '84* cap bobbed.

"Three for three's better than what *you* done in some time," grinned Buford. Buford was just as old as Cash—and though his jacket was denim instead of camo and his skin was white instead of brown, the two men could have been brothers.

Jack felt pretty sure they'd both been born old, ornery, and opinionated.

"Wasn't it you who missed that turkey out behind Morgan's field?"

"That was thirty years ago."

"Well, we all still talk about it."

"Who's 'we'?"

"Everyone."

"It was a hundred and fifty yards away... with turkey shot."

"Yeah, but you seemed *real* confident."

"Do y'all need me to work tomorrow morning?" Jack asked, interrupting the two old men, who stared at Jack as if they'd forgotten he was there.

When a boy is orphaned at a young age and frequently runs away from foster homes, he realizes the importance of money very quickly. As such, Jack had worked some job in some fashion since he was eight. Before he and Jimmy arrived in Opossum Trot, Jack sold newspapers and magazines, washed car windows, delivered food, and much more to help support himself and Jimmy.

When Ms. Dubois took them in, she insisted it wasn't necessary for him to keep working and stashing money. She told him to focus on school and baseball. But he got anxious when he didn't have at least some money coming in, so the second time she caught him collecting cans and scrap metal, Ms. Dubois compromised and got him some work with Buford and Cash.

Jack didn't know what "eccentric" meant when he first met Buford and Cash, but even if he had, he still would have just described them as crazy old men. When Ms. Dubois proposed the arrangement, she made it sound like he'd be doing odd jobs around their property. He expected mowing the fields, feeding the dozen or so goats they kept, and other hired-hand-type work.

On his first day, Buford asked Jack to get in the creek that ran along the east side of their property and check several snapping turtle traps. He failed to mention that the traps in question were live traps—or, that the traps were for *alligator* snapping turtles.

When Jack reached into the floating box-like contraption and almost lost a few fingers to a thirty-pound monster that looked like a cross between a turtle and a T-rex, he decided two things.

One, Buford and Cash were likely insane.

And two, he was probably going to enjoy his job.

Time proved him right on both counts. Buford and Cash had lived colorful lives, and they imparted a lot of wisdom and know-how in between their frequent spurts of bickering.

During the five years he'd helped out around their place, Jack learned how to operate a tractor, harvest crops, chop wood, and do pretty much everything else there was to do around the sprawling farm. Buford taught him how to fish, shoot guns, and trap game using homemade snares. Cash taught him how to swim, use camouflage, and track animals using his senses. All of which was initially foreign to a kid who'd never left the New Orleans city limits before coming to Opossum Trot. They even helped him improve his already-formidable fighting skills. And though Buford and Cash were outwardly gruff and quick to make sarcastic comments, Jack developed a real soft spot for them over time.

Lately, Jack focused on trying to cull the coyote population in the surrounding woods—Buford and Cash were having issues with goats and chickens being killed. But it seemed like for every wild dog Jack put down, two more sprang up, and he was starting to think his time would be better spent building more secure defenses around the coops and the barn. If he was being honest, he was tired of killing the coyotes, anyway. He related too much with the wiry scavengers.

"Won't you need some rest?" Cash asked. "I thought you kids stayed out all night doing that Challenge thing."

"I'll be fine to work, if you need me," Jack said, confidently.

He wasn't surprised they knew about the Challenge; it was an old tradition in Opossum Trot. Though no one knew exactly when it began, most of the other kids' parents could be caught talking about their childhood experiences with the town's spin on Halloween.

Local kids, mostly between the ages of ten and eighteen, would perform the scariest feats they could think to do, document them somehow, and compare notes to see whose exploits required the most bravery. Popular ventures included spending the night in the cemetery, bringing a souvenir back from the old, abandoned scrap yard, or climbing the water tower.

"What'd we do for that thing, again?" Buford asked Cash.

"Vietnam."

"Ah, that's right."

"So, about tomorrow?" Jack asked again, trying to head off whatever well-rehearsed war story was sure to follow.

"Yeah, come on by, if you want," Buford replied, waving a hand nonchalantly.

Jack nodded and handed the rifle to Cash.

Cash handed him three twenty-dollar bills with an approving nod. "Good work today, boy."

"I buried them at the edge of the woods."

"You could have just tossed them in the forest, nature'd take care of it," Cash said with a mildly puzzled look.

"Doesn't feel right."

"That's probably a good thing," Buford offered. "You go on home now. Give Renee our best."

Buford, Cash, and Mayor Dane were the only people in town who referred to Ms. Dubois by her first name. She was older than all of them, but they were all old enough to have known her when she was a young woman. To everyone else, Ms. Dubois was the town's surrogate grandmother. Professionally, she was the town's librarian, and generations of Opossum Trot citizens had all attended her weekly reading hours on Tuesday and Thursday afternoons.

Jack loved her—aside from his brother—more than anyone else in the entire world.

Δ

Neither Jack nor Jimmy remembered their parents. Neither knew anything about where they originally came from. Jack's earliest memory was of him and his brother being shuffled from foster home to foster home in New Orleans. Even their names had been assigned by the state. Jack asked about it once and was informed by their case worker that when the brothers were discovered living on the streets, they didn't have any records or identification, so they'd been designated "John Doe."

Apparently, this didn't sit well with whoever drew up their paperwork. The bureaucrat in question didn't like the idea of brothers having the same name. So, he changed the eldest Doe brother's name from "John" to "Jack." Then, reasoning it wasn't fair for only one brother to get a more unique name, the youngest brother had been dubbed "Jimmy." At least, that was the tale their case worker always told.

Jack and Jimmy came to live with Ms. Dubois because of an attempted theft. The brothers had a rich history of running away from group homes, particularly when child services tried to separate them. As such, they spent a lot of time living on their own, which required money to do safely. Jack's meager income provided a little, but not enough to support the two of them and bribe motel clerks for spare rooms. They occasionally had to use creative problem solving in order to make ends meet. One frequent fallback was selling "used" tires to Carlos Hernandez of Hernandez Tires. Carlos was always willing to put up a little cash for a lightly used, tier-one tire, and he never asked the two underage boys how they were able to come by so many.

On one particular day, Jack was removing the rear, driver-side tire from a Ford F150 when he sensed someone standing over his shoulder. Jimmy was supposed to be on look-out, and when Jack whirled around, he did see Jimmy—but he also saw a tall, gray-haired man. His brother wore a sheepish expression, but Jack's eyes fixed elsewhere.

The gray-haired man held his brother tightly by the collar. "Is he with you?"

Jack was eleven at the time, but he took a firm step toward the man. His knuckles were white from gripping the tire iron.

"Get your hand off my brother."

The tall man stared at Jack for a moment, then looked back down at Jimmy. To Jack, the man moved like a cop. He seemed to analyze the situation, to scan every detail about the two boys. Jack noticed the man's eyes resting on his shoes: a pair of black, off-brand Converses held together by superglue and duct tape.

Jack gritted his teeth and prepared to knock the man's hand loose from Jimmy, grab his brother, then run—when, to his surprise, the man smiled.

He let go of Jimmy and nodded at a diner up the street. "You boys want lunch?"

Before Jack could say anything, his brother blurted out, "Can I get fries? With chili and cheese?"

Jack glared at Jimmy, but then, he glanced at the man to see what he'd say.

"If it's okay with your brother."

Then, Jack took his own turn to play analyst. In his short but unfortunately extensive experience, there were few good Samaritans in the world who offered help without ulterior motives. At best, adults looking to "help" typically contacted DHS and got them sent back to a group home, and at worst… well, Jack didn't like to think about the worst-case scenarios.

But something about this guy seemed different to Jack. He was clean and neat, but he dressed in fancy clothes that didn't look quite comfortable for him. His hands were the hands of a worker or a fighter. His green eyes seemed intense and discerning but also kind. Jack thought the man was dangerous—but maybe not to him and Jimmy.

Jack didn't relax, but he felt himself nod. After all, they hadn't eaten anything besides microwavable noodles and corn chips in two days.

The man turned out to be the mayor of a small town called Opossum Trot, about an hour outside of the city and across the state line in Mississippi. His name was Hank Dane. He didn't bother asking if the boys were homeless or about what happened to their parents. He did ask about the group home. And Jack told him the truth.

The more they spoke, the more both brothers knew the man was decent.

Mayor Dane asked if they would be interested in a safe place, if it meant leaving the city.

They didn't say anything.

So, he told them about a nice older woman he thought would be willing to foster them. He promised they would be well taken care of, and they wouldn't have to worry about finding a place to stay or depending on strangers for food.

Jack would never forget how his brother looked at him then. His expression was a question that radiated hope.

Jack told himself he said yes to Mayor Dane just because he didn't have it in him to ruin that look. But he wondered. He wondered if, deep down, he knew he and Jimmy had been weirdly lucky. Lucky to manage as well as they had for so long, without starving or being hurt by someone cruel. He wondered if living beyond his maturity for so long had taken its toll—if he was simply exhausted.

Whatever the reason, Jack told Mayor Dane they'd be interested.

But he tried not to get his hopes up.

He needn't have worried. Mayor Dane did contact DHS, staying with the boys every step of the way as he arranged their new foster home. The boys found out that, before he became a mayor, Hank Dane served as a sheriff for almost thirty years. Jack got the impression that he had to call in some big, interstate favors to get everything worked out, but within two weeks, the boys' case worker dropped them off at a big, old house in Opossum Trot, Mississippi, where a kind woman greeted them with the worst cookies either boy had ever eaten.

A similar plate of cookies was offered to Jack when he walked into the same house after working for Buford and Cash. Ms. Dubois smiled so earnestly at Jack that he took two of the small, hard circles, just as he had done almost every day since that first. He crunched determinedly on the "treat" and thanked her.

Jack once met a guidance counselor who really loved the phrase, "No one's perfect." The counselor used it to remind Jack that he shouldn't be too judgmental of the foster parents he frequently fled. Though Jack still thought the guidance counselor was an out-of-touch tool, he did agree with the general sentiment of the phrase. The way he saw it, Ms. Dubois's baked goods were the only thing keeping her from complete perfection.

She hugged him after setting down the plate of cookies, the top of her head barely reaching Jack's chest. As usual, Ms. Dubois smelled like a pleasant mix of peanut butter and dish soap. Her light brown skin had a charmingly weathered quality to it, and she kept her gray hair cut short.

Jack gently hugged her back. She had been looking frail lately and moved with an unsteady shuffle when she walked. This development concerned Jack greatly.

"Did the boys have any work for you today?" she asked.

Jack smiled at the thought of anyone referring to Buford and Cash as "boys."

"Yes, ma'am. More coyotes."

"Oh, hon, that's going to give you nightmares," she said, sounding concerned.

"Nightmare," said Jack, overly pronouncing the end.

"Nonetheless."

Ms. Dubois was the only person on earth besides Jimmy who knew about the Nightmare. It was Jack's most shameful secret. It tended to occur at least once a month, but sometimes more often. Certain activities triggered it. Odd activities, though, like full moons, loud noises—and chocolate bars, for some reason. Most recently, the Nightmare was brought on by culling coyotes for Buford and Cash, a task they'd been assigning him more regularly in recent weeks.

Jack absolutely hated having the Nightmare, but a job was a job, and he took his work seriously.

Changing the subject, he asked, "Is Jimmy back yet?"

"He's in his room. I think he's brainstorming for tonight."

"Why? We already decided on staying the night in Nebelwood."

"I don't like that, Jack. You know how bad the hogs are. Besides, Jimmy said someone else is already doing that this year."

"I'll go talk to him."

"Y'all don't stay in that forest tonight, Jack. I'm serious. People have gotten hurt there." She gave Jack her *I-mean-it* look.

Jack returned the stubborn gaze for a moment, then sighed.

"Yes, ma'am."

Δ

Ms. Dubois's home was one of the oldest buildings in Opossum Trot, and she was the fourth generation of her family to live an entire life in their ancestral home. On the Does' way to meet Ms. Dubois for the first time, Mayor Dane told Jack and Jimmy all about the history of the large house. When the boys arrived, they realized the house was less Wayne-Manor and more Hill-House, minus the ghosts. It was a massive wooden structure that creaked constantly and had clearly been constructed prior to modern safety standards.

The Does loved it.

For two kids who never had anywhere they considered their real home, having their own rooms in a big, albeit-old house was incredible. Ms. Dubois gave them several options when it came to picking bedrooms, but the boys quickly settled on two rooms across from each other on the second floor. Jimmy wanted to share a room with Jack, but they compromised by sleeping with the doors open and talking loudly across the hallway. Ms. Dubois never complained, and the boys loved her all the more.

Jack strolled into Jimmy's room and took a seat at his brother's desk.

Jimmy sat on the floor of his closet with a pen and notebook. The youngest Doe brother typically gravitated to small, cozy spaces when he needed to brainstorm. He had a thoughtful expression on his face, and he didn't make any sign of acknowledging Jack.

Jack took issue with this, so he threw a slinky at him. The slinky knocked the notebook out of his brother's hand, making him flinch slightly.

Jimmy grunted exasperatedly, glared at his brother, and retrieved the notebook.

"Nice. Maybe instead you could help me think of something awesome for tonight."

"I'd rather not do it," said Jack, picking up a silver dollar that sat on the desk. "Ms. Dubois doesn't want us camping in the forest, and that would be the only fun thing."

"We need to do something different. Kids have been doing that one for years."

"How'd you hide your eye when you came in?" Jack asked, rolling the coin across his knuckles.

"Kept my head turned. Come on, seriously. We need to do something really scary, like Scott," Jimmy said, chewing contemplatively on the pen.

Two years prior, the boys' friend Scott Eldridge made local history with his answer to the Challenge—which surprised just about everyone. Scott was between the brothers in age, and though they both got along well with him, he was kind of an awkward kid: short and a little pudgy, stammering when he spoke, and never making eye contact with people. He only really got excited about anime and chess—mostly the latter. He always carried around a box with a folded chess board and a set of game pieces. Scott was the last kid anyone expected to go over the top with the Challenge.

But two years prior on Halloween, Scott went marching into the Nebelwood Forest. Instead of camping on the outskirts, as many kids had done over the years, Scott kept walking deeper and deeper until he found the ruins of The Mother's House.

Long before the boys moved there, a woman lived in an abandoned mansion deep in the forest. A drifter who became a bit of a local hero found the house, and he discovered what had been taking place there. She'd kidnapped several children over the years, and she'd kept them imprisoned in the basement. The woman—nicknamed "The Mother" by the town's storytellers, who viewed themselves more like historians—supposedly died during the encounter, but her body was never recovered. The police never released the actual location of the house, so many kids developed elaborate urban legends and often speculated about finding it.

But Scott actually did it. He found the house, and he stayed there by himself all night. His own mother eventually found a note saying what he planned on doing. The Sherriff and her deputy recovered Scott safely in the early hours of the following morning. Supposedly, he was found sitting calmly on the stairs of the basement, playing chess by himself. He'd gotten in a lot of trouble with his mom, but he'd achieved Halloween Challenge immortality.

Jack flipped the silver dollar into the air, leaned back, and let it land over his closed right eye.

"That wasn't a game. He'd just lost his dad."

Jimmy didn't say anything.

Jack saw the dejected look in his eyes, and he relented. "You're going about it wrong. Don't just think scary, think unknown. This town has other mysteries."

Jimmy furrowed his brow thoughtfully, then his eyes widened.

"What do you know about Old Man Porter?"

# CHAPTER THREE

Everyone in town knew of William Porter, even if no one knew him well. He had been the town mortician longer than anyone could remember, and though he attended almost every public gathering—particularly the annual crawfish boil—he was never actively involved with the other townsfolk. He seemed more a part of the setting of Opossum Trot than an actual resident. But it was hard not to notice him. He was tall, and though he looked almost as old as Ms. Dubois, he had lean, ropy muscles. He always wore jeans, a black t-shirt, and a matching flat-cap. Many in the community had also noticed strange tattoos on the palms of his hands.

But what really made Mr. Porter so striking wasn't his appearance, but the company he kept. He was never seen without Ceri.

Ceri was a dog—in the same sense that King Kong was a gorilla. She was larger than any other dog in town and, standing on her back legs, she almost reached the height of a grown man. She had a muscular frame that seemed perfectly balanced between wolf and bear. Her ears were large and stood straight up. She had an angular head, with the distinctive look of a predator.

But when people saw her, they mostly just saw darkness. Her fur was thick and the color of burnt shadow. Her eyes matched her fur. The only break in the darkness came when she opened her mouth to reveal large, ivory-colored teeth.

The people in town who particularly liked Ms. Dubois's library whispered that "Ceri" must be short for "Cerberus."

Ceri was well-behaved, though. She silently escorted William Porter wherever he went, on the few occasions that he left his funeral parlor. No one could remember her biting anyone, but most people didn't rush to pet her, either. On one occasion, at a May Day festival, a visitor to Opossum Trot had gotten inebriated and stumbled into William Porter. The mortician hadn't been irritated, but the visitor was embarrassed.

To cover his embarrassment, the visitor elected to push William Porter.

Ceri did not growl or flash her teeth.

Instead, the massive black dog stepped firmly between her master and the visitor, and she stared. Even in his drunken state, the man found it prudent to back away—slowly—and conclude with his festivities for the day.

Jimmy remembered that story when Jack suggested capitalizing on the town's other mysteries. He'd always wondered about the unusual funeral home director, but besides the story about Ceri and the May Day festival, there were few other known instances of anyone interacting with Old Man Porter. He helped with planning the occasional funeral, and that was it.

But Jimmy did know one other thing about the mysterious man. He'd heard it from Scott.

Jack and Jimmy and their group of friends were walking from school to the lone burger place in town, with him and Scott at the back of the group. Jimmy was sharing his extensive views on the quality of various English-dubbed Japanese cartoons.

As they passed by a dirt road that led to the town funeral home, Scott pointed it out to Jimmy. Then, the short, bespectacled boy said, "You know there's a locked shed behind the mortician's house."

By that point, Jimmy had grown used to Scott sharing random pieces of information, seemingly unrelated to any topic at hand. He usually just ran with it. "Oh yeah?"

"I saw it when we picked out my dad's coffin."

"What do you think's in it?"

"Well, my dad," said Scott, raising an eyebrow.

"Not the coffin. What do you think is in the shed?" said Jimmy, patiently.

"I don't know. But the lock looked weird."

"Weird how?"

Scott didn't say anything else about it, so Jimmy continued sharing his views on English-dubbed anime. In fact, Jimmy hadn't thought much about the conversation at all, until Jack prompted him.

Jack raised an eyebrow skeptically, but Jimmy's wheels kept turning.

"We need to find out what's in William Porter's creepy old shed," he told Jack.

"We don't even know if there *is* a creepy old shed. All we've got to go on is Scott."

"Are you saying Scott made it up?" Jimmy asked.

Jack didn't say anything. Despite all of Scott's quirks, he wasn't a liar, and Jack knew that.

Jimmy tried to seize the opportunity. He knew the only chance to convince Jack was to persuade him before he made up his own mind.

"We could pick the lock, take a picture, and be home before midnight. Think about it, a mortician with a giant dog who no one knows anything about? Even if we just find gardening tools, it would still win, just because we had the nerve to check it out."

"And what if we actually find something?"

"Bring the Heaven Breaker!"

Jack sighed, got to his feet, and walked to Jimmy's bed, plopping down without answering. Jimmy knew he would be asleep in seconds.

Jimmy took that as a good sign, though—it meant his brother wanted to get rest ahead of a long night.

The youngest Doe brother smiled in triumph.

As Jack began to snore softly, Jimmy leaned back and thought about the upcoming Challenge. He would need a camera and a flashlight, and they would probably need to borrow some bolt-cutters from Buford and

Cash, just in case the lock was too tricky. Jimmy doubted that, though. He'd gone through a Houdini phase, and Jack encouraged him to do something practical with the obsession—like learning to pick locks.

His older brother always opposed hobbies that didn't have practical applications. Their lives before Opossum Trot required them to possess a variety of self-sufficient skills and abilities, and lock picking helped the brothers find secure-if-unorthodox accommodations. During their times away from group homes, Jimmy gained entrance to a number of facilities, including an upscale townhouse whose owner was on vacation and an unoccupied floor of a high-rise corporate building.

Jack suddenly flinched violently in his sleep, returning his brother to the present. Jimmy watched, knowing what would come next.

Without waking up, his brother suddenly clenched his teeth in a violent grimace and swiped at something invisible.

Jimmy sighed. He was very familiar with his brother's Nightmare. He could probably choreograph every shudder, every twitch.

He got to his feet, stepped out of the closet, and walked toward the bed. He didn't wake his brother— that was dangerous. Instead, he just sat nearby and waited. He knew from experience that when Jack came out of his Nightmare, the first thing he'd do would be to look for Jimmy.

Jimmy smiled slightly.

He knew his brother was crazy, and he wouldn't have it any other way.

Δ

When the boys trooped down the stairs later that evening, Ms. Dubois greeted them, smiling and holding their coats. Neither boy commented on the fact that it was seventy-five degrees outside. Jimmy noticed her hand shake slightly when she handed them their jackets.

"No costumes tonight?" she asked.

"No ma'am," said Jimmy. Jack hated costumes—he always had.

"Well, what did y'all decide to do for the Challenge?"

"We're going to sneak into a creepy shed behind the funeral home," said Jack. As a rule, they never lied to Ms. Dubois.

"You mean at Mr. Porter's?" she asked.

"Yes ma'am," they said in unison.

"Such a strange man. You know, I think I have a picture of him somewhere." Ms. Dubois started toward the living room, where she kept her boxes of photographs.

"We'll probably be late," said Jack, over his shoulder.

"We'll bring you back some candy!" Jimmy added, following his brother.

As the door closed behind the boys, Ms. Dubois pulled a shoebox out from a cabinet in the living room, then scanned the assorted photographs it contained.

Her gaze lingered on a faded polaroid of a startlingly young Buford and Cash in military dress uniforms, but she eventually picked up the picture underneath. She placed the picture in the pocket of her dress and made a mental note to show it to the boys later.

If the Doe brothers had seen the picture, they likely would not have changed their plans for the evening.

But perhaps they would have been a little better prepared.

# CHAPTER FOUR

Jack strolled with Jimmy up Main Street in downtown Opossum Trot. The smattering of shops and stores were all decorated with Jack-o-lanterns, hanging papier-mâché skeletons, and cardboard cutouts placed in windows to look like monstrous shapes lurking in the darkness. Flickering candles inside the carved pumpkins cast a warm but mischievous glow over the small, bustling street. Though the Challenge was a major event for older children in Opossum Trot, Halloween was still Halloween, and almost all the businesses on Main Street handed out treats to diminutive monsters, cartoon characters, and superheroes.

The eldest Doe brother adjusted a duffel bag on his shoulder. On their way into town, the two boys stopped by Buford and Cash's to borrow supplies—adding two high-powered flashlights, two pairs of night-vision goggles, and bolt cutters to the bag with Jimmy's lock pick set and a small Tupperware of Ms. Dubois's cookies.

Jack doubted they would need the bolt cutters; few locks gave his brother trouble anymore.

"Looks like Claire is already here," said Jimmy, grinning, and Jack bristled.

A small group of people mingled ahead of them. Eric and Thomas were White boys in most of Jimmy's classes at school. Their parents ran adjoining soy farms on the west side of town, and they were largely insepa-rable. Amelia was in Jack's grade. She was a short, slim Latina who—for reasons no one seemed to under-stand—had a major crush on Scott and always fiercely protected the awkward chess aficionado. Scott, on the other hand, seemed oblivious to how she felt. Claire was an athletic Black girl with long, natural hair, which she usually wore pulled back in a headband. She was taller than everyone else in the group.

Claire always seemed happy to see Jack—especially since the Fourth of July carnival—and Jimmy liked to joke about it.

Jack hadn't planned for the carnival to turn out the way it did. He, Jimmy, and their friends all decided to go together. Jack hadn't particularly wanted to ride the Ferris wheel, but somehow, he ended up alone in a car with Claire. He didn't talk much as the ride started, but neither did Claire, which surprised him. He nor-mally found it easy to talk to her, partially because she was willing to hold up his side of the conversation.

He looked over to check on her, and he was sur-prised to find her sitting with her eyes closed and taking deep, nervous breaths. Then Jack remembered: she didn't like heights.

Jack shuffled uncomfortably in his seat for a mo-ment. Then, he reached over and gently took her hand. He hated the idea of her being scared, even if it was just over a stupid ride. But he couldn't look at her, either—he still wasn't sure why.

After a few nervous moments, Claire squeezed his hand.

As the giant metal wheel slowly turned, Jack noticed her breathing return to normal, and through his peripheral vision, he saw her eyes open.

But he didn't let go of her hand. He liked the feeling, to his own surprise, and maintained his hold on her for the entire ride.

They hadn't spoken of it. But after that night, she always smiled when she saw him.

Claire, true to form, grinned when they approached, and she was the first to say hi to Jack.

Jack nodded in what he hoped was a polite manner, but Jimmy rolled his eyes and went to greet Eric and Thomas.

After everyone exchanged greetings, the group began walking and talking.

"Did you and Jack really beat up Miles, Keegan, and the Davises?" Eric asked Jimmy.

"Not exactly," Jimmy said, shooting a quick glare at his brother. "I only fought Miles, and he'd been damaged already."

"Still—" Thomas interjected, "—I heard both Keegan and Miles aren't coming out tonight because they're afraid of Jack."

Jack smirked.

Claire changed the subject. "So, what's everyone doing for the Challenge?"

"We're gonna try to find something weird at the scrapyard," said Eric.

"You know they have junkies that camp out there?" said Jimmy, raising an eyebrow.

"That's what makes it scary," replied Thomas. "What are y'all doing?"

"We're going to break into the locked shed behind the funeral home."

"That's new," said Eric, approvingly.

"Just don't let Mr. Porter catch you. That dude's dog is freakier than any junkie," said Amanda, shaking her head matter-of-factly.

"I've always thought she was really pretty," said Claire.

"I guess…"

"Well, this is us," said Eric, when they reached the dirt road that eventually led to the scrapyard. "Y'all try not to get killed." Then, he and Thomas parted from the group.

Amanda and Claire walked with Scott and the Doe brothers a little farther, until they came to the path that led to the town cemetery. There, the girls turned away, leaving just the Doe brothers and Scott to walk down the dark, country road.

"How is Ms. Dubois?" asked Scott, breaking the silence.

"Why?" asked Jack.

"She used to do reading time every Saturday when I was little. Then, it was every other week. Now, she only does it once a month."

"She's just been a little tired," said Jimmy, quickly, not wanting his brother to take any offense.

But Jack said nothing; he wouldn't have admitted it to Scott or even to Jimmy, but he'd been worried about Ms. Dubois for some time.

They walked on in silence for a few minutes. Then, Scott changed the subject.

"I don't think y'all should do this."

"What, the Challenge?" Jimmy asked.

"You should pick something else." Scott stared down at his feet, but he spoke clearly and with an unfamiliar tone of warning.

"Why?" Jimmy asked.

"I don't think Mr. Porter is normal."

Jack perked up, pinning Scott with wary eyes. "What do you mean? Is he bad?"

"I don't think so. But after my dad… Well, we spoke to Mr. Porter a couple times, when we made arrangements. I'd never spoken to him before. I don't think my parents had either."

"So?"

"He just seemed to know a lot about my dad. Recent stuff. The kind of stuff we got in letters, right before."

The brothers didn't say anything. This was the most Jack had heard Scott talk about his father since before the funeral. The Does only knew Drew Eldridge had been in the military and died suddenly, in an accident somewhere in the Middle East.

Eventually, Scott cleared his throat.

"I just think Mr. Porter is different, somehow. The other stuff, like the Mother's house, the forest, the cemetery, they're scary. But they're just empty places. They haven't really been dangerous in years."

"What are you saying?" prodded Jimmy.

"I wish I hadn't told you about that locked shed. I think whatever someone like Mr. Porter is guarding, it's probably very dangerous."

Jack looked at Jimmy, who seemed a little disturbed by Scott's words. He patted his brother's shoulder and grinned. "We can be dangerous too."

Scott sighed, but he didn't say anything else. When they reached the fork in the road that led to the funeral home, Scott paused. For the first time that evening, he raised his head and looked directly at the brothers. His gaze settled on Jack.

"When you play chess, you rely on your queen too much."

Jack was used to Scott's scattered way of talking—he was also used to this particular criticism.

Whenever they played chess, Jack tended to favor his queen. He mostly used the other pieces just to set up sweeping attacks that gradually ate away at his opponents' forces. Scott thought this was lazy, and he often tried to introduce Jack to more complex strategies.

In their most recent game, Scott only used his knights, working in tandem to dismantle Jack's attacks and achieving a relatively quick checkmate. Jack was impressed with the gameplay, to the point where he even asked Scott to show him the basics of how it worked. Nonetheless, Jack still favored a direct approach using his queen.

"It's the strongest piece," Jack replied.

"Even the strongest piece needs help to win the game." Scott held out a closed hand to Jack.

Jack raised an eyebrow, but he extended his hand.

Scott dropped something into his palm. When Jack looked down, he saw an ivory chess piece: a knight.

"It was my dad's. Take it for luck tonight."

With that, Scott turned around and began walking home in the dark. Jack and Jimmy exchanged a look, shrugged, and began walking up the turn-off that led to the funeral home.

Jack took one of the flashlights from the duffel bag and turned it on. He cupped his hand over the front so that only a small amount of light could escape at a downward angle, allowing the brothers to see where they were walking without sending the beam toward the funeral parlor.

The Opossum Trot Funeral Home was actually a small, two-story antebellum home with a wraparound porch and balcony. The building was scenic and aged, except for a modern-looking addition on the eastern side with a sterile, utilitarian quality. Jack guessed Porter kept the bodies there. Pine trees surrounded the house, and as the boys approached, they stayed low and stuck to the wood line. Eventually, they settled in a particularly tight crop of trees and opened the duffel bag again.

Jack pulled out the two pairs of night vision goggles and handed one pair to Jimmy. When Jack switched his on, the world turned from black to electric green. There was no moon that night, and there weren't any porch lights on, so Jack had a clear picture of the entire property, including the mysterious utility shed just to the right at the back of the house. Even better, he could see two shapes through the window of the second story bedroom.

"That must be him and the dog," said Jimmy.

"Yeah. How quickly do you think you can make it across the yard?"

Without another word, Jimmy took off toward the side of the house closest to the shed.

Jack swung the duffel bag over his shoulder. He kept his eyes on the window to make sure Mr. Porter and his dog didn't change positions, and he darted after Jimmy. As he slid against the eastern side of the house, he scanned the area. There was no movement in his field of vision, and he couldn't hear any alarmed noises coming from inside the house.

"I need my lock pick."

Jack held a finger to his lips and furrowed his brow at his brother. Then, he reached into the bag again and handed the black case containing the picks to Jimmy. Motioning for him to lean close, Jack cupped his hands around his mouth and whispered softly, "Move quietly. I'll keep lookout. If I whistle, run. Meet me at home."

Jimmy nodded and crept across the yard to the old utility shed.

Jack watched him go for a second, then glanced around the corner of the house so he had a clear view of the front door. He watched the door for the slightest tremble and kept his ears primed for any sudden stirring. When he glanced back at Jimmy, his brother pulled two thin slivers of metal from the case and inserted them into the lock. Even from a distance, the lock looked oversized and antique.

Both brothers were practiced lookouts. When Mayor Dane caught Jimmy during the would-be tire heist, he broke a long streak of over thirty successful jobs by the youngest Doe. Though everything worked out in the end, Jack still gave Jimmy a hard time for being noticed.

Jack's perfect record ended just as abruptly.

The low growl of an immense beast suddenly reverberated in Jack's ear and echoed throughout his entire frame.

His head swung up and to the side, still wearing the night vision goggles. In the dark, he saw a monstrous shadow peel back its lips, exposing two rows of impossibly large teeth.

Jack tensed, but the lupine monster wasn't interested in him.

It was staring at Jimmy.

Before Jack could whistle, the animal leapt over him toward his brother. Jack instinctively lunged forward. In his desperate effort, he managed to catch one of the creature's hind legs.

He thought the oversized dog would turn and snap at him, but she was laser-focused on Jimmy, and she ignored Jack while straining against his grip.

Jack gritted his teeth and pulled, but the beast dragged him forward, nonetheless.

Jimmy turned one of the metal slivers sharply and tugged on the old lock. He seemed oblivious to the chaos unfolding behind him.

"What the— let go of her!" boomed a voice from behind.

A firm hand yanked Jack backward, away from the dog. Jack instinctively rolled his shoulder and took a swing at whoever grabbed him.

Jack couldn't make out the man's features, but he was clearly tall and fast, managing to slip past Jack's punch and hit him with a hard palm in the ribs. Jack raised his hands, ready for a fight, eyes on the man's shadowed face.

But his attacker wasn't looking at him, either.

He was staring at Jimmy.

The dog bounded toward the youngest Doe brother, who still didn't notice anything behind him.

His attention was fixed on the lock that lay open in his hand, the heavy chain it once held already fallen onto the ground.

Jimmy pulled the iron bar free from the handles, then turned triumphantly toward his brother. And for the first time, he saw the man and the giant dog.

Jack heard Mr. Porter whisper, "What have you done?" Then, he yelled, "GET AWAY FROM THE—"

But the twin doors of the old shack shot open, striking Jimmy and forcing him off his feet.

The hiss of wind rushing like a gas leak filled the air. Light burst from the darkness of the shed and illuminated the entire property.

Jack whipped off his goggles and crawled toward his brother, but the light was so bright, he had to squint and raise a hand to shield his eyes. He heard Mr. Porter bellow in his direction, but the man's ranting mattered nothing to Jack.

He had to get to Jimmy.

The familiar panic he associated with the Nightmare enveloped him as he fumbled blindly forward. The powerful light flickered, and strange shadows emerged from the shed.

Jack craned his neck and tried to look at one of the shadows through his fingers. A vaguely human shape loomed over him—a cloud of dark vapor that lacked much definition.

The shape seemed to stare back. Then, it reached toward him.

But Mr. Porter stepped over Jack and caught the shape—by the closest thing it had to a neck—and hurled it back into the blinding void of light emanating from the old shack.

Without pause, Mr. Porter reached toward another dark figure trying to bolt past him. This figure was a little less abstract: a young man in a camouflage jacket. Mr. Porter caught him by his arm and slung him off his feet into the streaming light. As the young man's dark form dissolved into the brightness, Mr. Porter's palms glowed.

Before Jack could wonder at the impossibility of anything, he heard snarling and rolled to his left. The massive black dog dragged another shadowy, clawing form back toward the entrance of the shed.

But then, Jack heard Jimmy cry, "Help!"

Jack looked back and froze.

A hand reached from inside the old shack, grasping Jimmy by the leg of his jeans. The hand was large and bony, and its elongated, spiderlike fingers fully encircled Jimmy's ankle. Even from a distance, Jack could see sharp, uneven fingernails cutting into denim. The hand was attached to a thin, pale arm that rippled with lean muscle, yanking Jimmy backward into the powerful light.

Jack heard himself roar, "No!" as he frantically crawled forward.

Jimmy's face was a mask of panic, his body quickly disappearing into the glowing shed despite all efforts to claw into the ground.

Jack drew his feet under him and lunged forward, reaching both hands out toward his brother. His right hand caught Jimmy by the wrist, and Jack quickly reinforced his grip with his left hand before pulling as hard as he could.

"Don't let go!" he yelled, straining to pull his brother free from the otherworldly grip.

The pale hand's grasp only tightened.

Jimmy's pained cries made Jack wince, but he gritted his teeth and pulled, straining until he felt like the muscles in his arms and back would tear.

It wasn't enough. The pale arm jerked sharply, and Jimmy sank deeper into the blinding light.

Jack's grasp slipped, until he only held his brother's fingertips. He tried desperately to adjust his grip, but it was no use.

With one last scream, Jimmy disappeared completely into the glowing void. Malicious cackling mingled in with his fading screams.

The sudden imbalance in force sent Jack flying backward. He hit the ground hard, and his head slammed against the tightly packed dirt. As blackness engulfed his mind, he saw one last strange image.

William Porter stepped over his prone form and tried to wrestle the door shut against the rush of wind and light. A figure stood in the door frame, about Jack's height, but not as broad. He wore jeans, boots, and an olive-colored canvas jacket that almost reached his knees. His face was obscured by a plastic fox mask.

As Jack blacked out, the specter with the fox face stared at him.

# CHAPTER FIVE

For all the fear and anxiety that it caused Jack, the Nightmare never lasted long.

The Doe brothers run through the woods on a dark night.

At first, Jack can't see what's pursuing them. But he can hear it, right from the start. The roar fills the air, completely obscuring any words exchanged by the fleeing brothers.

Then, the darkness brightens, and in true panic, Jack gapes at the loud, furious thing chasing him and Jimmy.

It's made of light. As if all the shine from all the stars and from the moon itself has condensed into one monstrous form, with glowing claws and teeth all searching hungrily for the fleeing children.

Suddenly, Jimmy trips—sometimes on a rock, other times on a root, but always at the worst possible second. Jack skids to a halt, but not soon enough, always becoming separated from his brother by a few yards.

The monster falls upon the youngest Doe before Jack can reach him.

Jack screams and rushes toward his brother, flinging himself violently at the creature, but the monster engulfs Jimmy and roars. It rears up, growing, expanding until it is everywhere, until the woods disappear into its impossible glow.

Jack is already in the air when he realizes he has leapt headfirst into the maw of the beast.

From his elevated vantagepoint, Jack sees the partially devoured remains of his brother, skewered in teeth made of light. And Jack's screams of anger turn to terror.

Then Jack wakes up, fists clenched and heart thumping like it's about to burst. He is covered in sweat and breathing heavily. But as he wakes, remembers, and acclimates to reality, there is always an eventual moment of peculiar peace.

But on the morning after that Halloween, he did not feel the familiar peace and calm—either because reality had become as frightening as the Nightmare, or because when he opened his eyes, Jack found himself lying on an embalming table.

"You awake?"

Jack sat up and whirled around.

William Porter waited on a nearby stool. The mortician wore the same clothes from the previous night, but he held a Sudoku booklet and a pencil.

Jack's gaze lingered on the game for a moment, then he launched himself off the table, directly at William Porter.

The giant, black dog hit him midair and drove him to the floor—so hard, Jack lost his breath momentarily. When he opened his eyes, Jack lay on his back, staring up into a very imposing set of teeth.

William Porter never flinched. He placed the pencil behind his ear, stood up, and shoved the puzzle booklet into his back pocket. "You ought to calm down. We don't have time for histrionics."

"Where's my brother?!" Jack roared, ignoring the dog looming over him.

"Not sure," Mr. Porter shrugged. "Somewhere bad though. And he's going to be stuck there forever, unless you sober up."

His attention captured, Jack took a deep breath and forced himself to stay calm.

"You good?" The mortician's voice was firm but not antagonistic.

Jack didn't say anything—he stared at the old man in disbelief.

"Fair enough. Now, I'm guessing you and that other boy, your brother, didn't expect all that to happen when you opened my shed?"

Jack shook his head.

"I'm thinking you two were probably doing that asinine Halloween Challenge that people do around here. Or just generally being idiot children?"

Jack nodded. The unfavorable assessment seemed fair to him, all things considered.

"Well, congratulations. You and your brother are the most pigheaded fools that have ever been through this whole fool town, and he's probably going to die."

Jack just stared at him, disbelieving, waiting.

Eventually, Mr. Porter sighed. "It didn't occur to you that if a door is chained shut, maybe there's a reason for it?"

"Clearly not."

William Porter barked a humorless laugh. He snapped his fingers, and the dog removed her front paw from Jack's chest.

Jack sat up on his elbows and glared at the old man, who shrugged.

"Well, as you probably guessed, that's not just a utility shed out there."

"Where does it go?"

"The Hinderwood."

Jack waited.

"All you need to know is there are places in this world where the veil is thin. Where the barriers that separate our world from others is almost non-existent. That old shed is one of those places."

"Where does it go?" Jack repeated in disbelief.

"Limbo. The hereafter. I've always called it the Hinderwood, but basically it's where you go before whatever lies— beyond."

Jack tried to make sense of Porter's explanation, but either because he'd recently been knocked unconscious or because the general strangeness of the past few hours was too much to comprehend, Jack failed to process any of it.

Then, he remembered something from the night before. Something that made even less sense.

"What were those things that came out? Those… shadows?"

"The lost ones. Spirits that weren't ready for what comes next. Some have been waiting so long, they've forgotten what they're waiting for. But over time, without purpose, they fade … or they feed."

"Feed?" Jack felt his head swimming.

"On life. Even the dead have a little life still lingering in their spirits. So, some turn predator. They feed on other spirits or, if they get loose, the living."

"So, you think one of those took my brother?"

William Porter nodded.

"Then let's go get him." Jack didn't wholly understand or believe the mortician's explanation, but he was, at heart, a pragmatist. He knew instinctively what to do.

When he got to his feet, Ceri allowed it but stayed nearby and didn't take her eyes off him.

William Porter shook his head.

"People don't just go walking into the edge of Hell." William pointed in the general direction of the shed. "Before you two came along, that door hadn't been opened in generations. To my knowledge, a regular, living, breathing human has never walked through, including myself. Besides, I won't leave my post."

"Why not?" Jack asked raising an eyebrow. "You can't just leave my brother down there."

"You're getting to peek behind the curtain a bit here, boy. Maybe just believe me when I say that there are details you don't need to fully understand."

"Fine, I'll go."

It was William Porter's turn to stare hard at Jack. Jack did not rattle, as a rule, but the mortician's dark eyes held something ancient and otherworldly, something that made him want to shudder in spite of himself.

Nonetheless, Jack didn't blink.

"Alright. But you need to understand, you're on your own in there. No one's coming in after you. You want to find your brother, it's up to you."

"Nothing new."

William Porter searched Jack's face, as if looking for some sign of doubt or fear. Seeing nothing, he sighed and continued. "Maybe, but you also need to know you're on a time limit."

"What?" asked Jack.

"A living being can only spend two days in the Hinderwood. After forty-eight hours, the gate won't let you back in... not as a human, anyways."

"So, he'd be a ghost?" inquired Jack, still bewildered and disbelieving.

"At first. But over time, most spirits without a tether go mad and start preying on the living. I'm afraid if you and your brother don't return within two days, I can't allow you back through the door."

Jack didn't say anything, but he reflected on what Scott said to him earlier. For a moment, he felt furious with himself for not heeding his friend's warning; however, he knew there was no time for dwelling on it. Regrets wouldn't bring his brother back.

He steeled himself and tried to focus on Mr. Porter.

"And, in case you didn't gather from last night's experience, you won't be safe once you cross that threshold. Most of the spirits in there are malicious, and even the ones that aren't can still get you killed."

"I'm not afraid."

"We'll see how far that gets you," Mr. Porter said, skeptically. "Anyways, if you're serious about going after him, you'd better get to it."

"I have to get some things first. I'll meet you back here in an hour." Jack moved toward the door marked "Exit."

"Remember," the old man called. "You've only got two days, and there's no telling how long it's going to take you on the other side."

Δ

Jack thought about going to the sheriff, but only for a couple seconds.

If what the old man said was true, he didn't have time to convince a cop to come check William Porter's shed for ghosts. If he was lying... well, at least there'd be time to figure that out.

Jack didn't think Porter was being deceitful, though—at least, not about what was in the old shack. He'd seen the shadow-like figures, how they desperately tried to escape the churning brilliance of light. Clearly, something unusual went on in that shed.

As he reflected on the previous night, Jack was surprised to find his thoughts lingering not on the aggressive, shadowy forms, or even on the pale arm that reached from the void, but on the still, calculating figure in the fox mask. There was something particularly disturbing about the curious eyes that watched him through that false face. Something almost familiar that he couldn't quite articulate.

He didn't go in the front door of Ms. Dubois's home. He didn't have time to explain everything to her, and he wouldn't lie, either. So, Jack stood on an overturned bucket at the side of the house and boosted himself into his bedroom.

Jack didn't waste any time. He'd forgotten his duffel bag at the funeral home, so he emptied his backpack of school books and filled it with his canteen, a first aid kit, some emergency glow-sticks, some MREs Buford once gave him, his leather jacket, a grappling hook Jimmy gave him for Christmas, a multi-tool, and some spare underwear and socks.

The last thing he did was pick up his bat and slide it into the special sleeve Ms. Dubois had sewn into the side of the pack. The familiar weight comforted him as much as a prayer—which made him feel a little guilty when he realized it.

He could hear Ms. Dubois moving around downstairs.

But Jack gave the room one last look, took a breath, and climbed back out the window.

He didn't return directly to the funeral home. He had one more stop to make. It was a long run, but eventually, he got where he needed to be.

Inches at a time, he made his way through the old barn toward a tall metal locker bolted to the south wall. He moved stealthily, trying to roll his feet so as not to make any sound. He didn't worry about the padlock on the door—Jack knew the key sat under a rusty pail, just a couple feet away. He'd put it there yesterday after work.

He retrieved it now and opened the locker.

"Don't need any varmint work today. But something tells me you got your own hunt planned."

Jack ignored the voice and opened his backpack. He filled it with two boxes of bullets and four empty magazines. After zipping up the bag and returning it to his shoulder, Jack pulled the 30.06 rifle from the locker and slung it over his other shoulder.

Once he was finished, he turned to face Buford. "I'll return it. And I'll pay y'all back for the bullets."

"Well, the fact that you plan on spending some is what concerns me," said Buford, raising a gray eyebrow.

"Jimmy's in trouble. It's hard to explain, but I need you to trust me," said Jack.

"Trust you to hurt the right people?" Buford asked, offering a humorless smile.

"Yes."

"That's not always an easy call to make."

"Nothing about this is going to be easy."

Buford chuckled. "Can't tell you how many times I've heard Cash say that."

"Are you going to stop me?"

Buford stepped past Jack and shut the locker. He replaced the lock and put the key back in its place, but he made no move to reclaim the gun. He looked Jack in the eye for a moment without saying anything.

Then, he grinned.

"You know how many times I've taken a gun and gone off to do something that needed doing? Stopped counting in '74. Naw, Jack, you're a good kid—a weird kid, but a good one. You proved yourself responsible long before you started hanging around us. Can I offer some wisdom, though?"

"Yes, sir."

His voice uncharacteristically stern, Buford said, "Once you pull a trigger, there's no putting the bullet back in the chamber."

Buford and Cash were careful and responsible— in their own unique way—and always approached the proper use of tools with a no-nonsense mentality. They taught Jack that a gun was a particularly serious tool.

So, Jack did not hesitate to answer in an equally serious tone, "I understand."

$$\Delta$$

When Jack arrived at the funeral home, he entered through the same side door he'd left earlier that morning. Once inside, he was surprised not to find William Porter and Ceri waiting for him. The sterile embalming room echoed slightly when he walked across the tile floors.

But he turned out not to be completely alone—he heard voices in the next room.

Jack moved as quietly as he could to the tall, swinging door on the opposite side of the room. When he put his eye up to the crack between the door and wall, he was treated to a narrow view of the display room for the coffins and flower arrangements.

A man in a dark suit faced Mr. Porter and Ceri. Because the man stood with his back to the door, Jack couldn't see any of his features, except for his suit and the briefcase he held.

William Porter focused intensely on their conversation, but beside him, Ceri cocked her head and looked directly at Jack.

Jack stepped away from the crack but kept listening.

"My task is to keep them from getting out, not to stop foolish children from going in," said Mr. Porter.

"As stated in the initial contract, your task is to— and I quote—'Act as the primary gatekeeper for Entry

Point No. 14, with duties including but not limited to: barring admittance to all non-native and non-corporeal entities, monitoring and reporting on any barrier expansion events, maintaining secrecy as required, and protecting any living beings at risk resulting from proximity to the site.'"

"That's what the chain was for," said William Porter, grudgingly.

"You will receive a formal warning for this infraction. You are fortunate that nothing escaped as a result of your negligence."

"This was my first issue since taking the position. No one has a record as clean as mine."

"Your historic diligence is noted. However, while you have been proficient in your duties, you have done little to elevate your position."

"I wasn't aware there were promotions."

"May I speak plainly?" Jack heard the click of dress shoes on the wooden floor.

"I have no idea. Can you?"

"You have been granted considerable personal resources related to your assignment, yet your situation is nearly identical to when you started."

"This town needed a mortician. Would you rather I ran a bed and breakfast?"

"I am not concerned with the location's secondary function."

"I do my job. And don't go forgetting that I didn't ask for this."

Jack heard nothing else for a full minute, until the sound of shuffling papers broke the silence.

"I know what you are planning. Jack Doe has little chance of success. Though I can confirm Jimmy Doe is still living, there is only a three percent chance of their safe return. Even if they do manage, the standard protocols cannot be ignored."

"What else would you have me do?"

"I would suggest remembering why you initially accepted this assignment."

"You don't know everything."

"My job is to know enough. Now, I believe Mr. Doe is ready for you."

Jack started in surprise. How had the man seen him? But it didn't matter. Sighing, he pushed the door open, ready to face the two men.

His surprise returned with an increase when he found the room empty except for William Porter and Ceri.

"Where'd the guy in the suit go?"

"Trust me when I say you should do everything in your power to forget about him." William Porter massaged his temples wearily. "I assume you're ready to go?"

"Yes."

"You should know that I agree with the man you should forget about. Your odds of survival are abysmal."

"Story of my life."

William Porter smiled in spite of himself. Then he led Jack and Ceri out of the funeral home toward the shed.

The chains were locked back into place with the strange padlock, but the mortician produced a small iron key that looked like something forged in the Middle Ages. "The spirits are less active during the day, but you'll still have only a second to enter. If I leave the door open for longer than a moment, they'll swarm."

"Okay."

"You should see the door on the other side, but I think it'll just be an empty frame," Mr. Porter explained. "Nothing will happen when you walk through unless I open it on this side. I can't leave it open, or it will attract others."

"How?"

"I've never been on the other side, but I've always gotten the sense it gives off a kind of beacon when opened. We'll do a test once you're on the other side, try to use it as a signal. You can use it to find your way back, if you find your brother."

"When," Jack corrected.

"Yes, when you find him." William Porter nodded at Jack's pack. "You have everything you need?"

"I think so."

"That gun probably won't help you much," he said, staring at the rifle.

"Whatever grabbed Jimmy was able to touch him. Stands to reason it can be touched, too."

"There's not much reason where you're going, kid," the mortician said, though he seemed thoughtful.

William Porter reached into his pocket and pulled out what looked to Jack like an old-fashioned pocket watch. After pressing the fob and clicking open the timepiece, he twisted a dial two times, inspected the face, and handed it to Jack.

The bronze timepiece turned out to be a kind of antique countdown timer, with turning white blocks ticking off different numbers: years, months, days, hours, minutes, and seconds.

Jack read, "One day, fifteen hours, and three minutes."

"That's how long you have to find your brother and get him back here."

"Don't suppose I can take the dog?" Jack nodded at the immense black dog pacing behind the mortician. "Seems like she's pretty good to have on your side."

"I need her here. You going after your brother is one thing, but my priority is keeping anything from escaping."

"Alright." Jack slid the timer into his pocket. "Let's do it."

"Knock twice to let me know the beacon works."

Without another word, William Porter swung the doors open. Light rushed out, but it wasn't as pronounced in the daytime.

Jack regarded the interior for a moment. The light was so bright, it was hard to gauge the depth of the shed. His pulse quickened, and he had to force his breathing to remain consistent. The familiar grip of terror that he associated with the Nightmare started to ensnare him.

But he didn't give it a chance.

Jack closed his eyes, whispered a quick prayer, and let himself fall forward.

Δ

William Porter snapped the door shut behind the boy. He waited for a long beat, then quickly opened and closed the door again, hopefully to illustrate the door's capability as a beacon. After a brief pause, he heard two sharp knocks from inside the shed.

That accomplished, William stared at the chain and lock for a moment, pondering. Right or wrong, he knew he had… various options.

But he felt judgmental eyes watching, and when he turned toward Ceri, she stared at him—quite disapprovingly.

He sighed. "Alright."

William Porter left the chains and lock on the ground, plopping down in his folding chair by the door. Ceri sat by his feet.

Together, they waited.

# INTERLUDE ONE: JIMMY

Everything would be okay. Jack would come for him, he would do the Look, and everything would be okay.

Jimmy reckoned that he knew his brother as well as he knew himself. That being said, his brother never seemed particularly complicated. He liked ancient history, working outside, and, recently, baseball. He disliked cluttered rooms, rudeness, and most people. Jack was often quiet, methodical, and prone to introspection. When angry, he was ferocious and brutal but never cruel. He could be surprisingly gentle and kind, especially with women and girls. Above all, Jack was loyal and protective. Jack would go to the ends of the earth for the few people who mattered to him.

Jimmy was counting on that.

Fortunately, Jack was remarkably consistent. Certain quirks of his could be counted upon almost invariably. Jimmy thought about one in particular, as the monster dragged him through the dark—specifically, he thought about the Look.

Jimmy first saw the Look when he was five years old, when they lived in their first group foster home in New Orleans—or at least, the first one Jimmy could remember clearly. The house belonged to an older couple named Jeff and Betty Albert. They were nice and warm, but several rough, older kids lived there who did not care for the Doe brothers.

A couple of those boys confronted Jack and Jimmy away from the watchful Alberts' supervision.

A mean-looking kid with a haircut he'd clearly given himself shoved an open palm under Jack's nose. "Y'all got any money?"

Jack said nothing. He held the mean kid's gaze calmly, reached into his pocket, and handed over a couple crumbled dollar bills.

A boy with braces and bushy eyebrows pointed at Jimmy. "What's he got?"

Jimmy had been holding nervously onto his rabbit's foot, and he quickly hid it behind his back.

"He doesn't have anything," said Jack.

The kid with the bad haircut pushed Jack, and the other one reached for Jimmy. "Hand it over!"

Jimmy tried to make himself small, but even in his cringing, he still saw Jack's eyes.

Jack stared at Jimmy, then the kid with the bad haircut, then the boy with braces, then Jimmy again.

That's when the Look started. It began with Jack's right hand, which balled into a white-knuckled fist. Next was a slight turn of the head, followed by a clenching of the jaw. The last stage happened in Jack's eyes, which narrowed into two slits of cold fury.

Taken together, the Look meant someone would soon learn the full extent of the damaged boy's capacity for violence.

Both Haircut and Braces were dealt swift and merciless lessons—and that ended Jack and Jimmy's stay at the Alberts'.

As something unknown dragged Jimmy roughly across an unfamiliar land, he prayed for the Look.

When he was pulled through the shed door into a strange, dark place, Jimmy did not see his captor. He'd been ripped away from his brother, so he started punching and kicking in every direction, just like Jack told him to do if any stranger ever grabbed him.

In this case, the stranger slapped him so hard, his vision blurred. Next thing he knew, he was shoved into a thick burlap sack. The sack quickly cinched shut, and his captor began dragging him along to some unknown destination.

Jimmy tried to speak to his kidnapper several times. First, he just cursed and threatened the being on the other side of the sack. When that earned him nothing but a sharp kick, he tried reasoning and bargaining, but his pleas only drew harsh laughter that made Jimmy cringe, the same way he'd cringe if a nail were dragged across a blackboard. Eventually, he grew silent and could only listen—to his captor singing softly to himself.

Jimmy didn't panic though. Jack was going to come for him sooner or later, and he wouldn't hear the end of it if he didn't at least make a go of rescuing himself.

He looked around and performed a quick inventory. He'd lost his night vision goggles. However, the small metal flashlight was still in his back pocket along with his rabbit's foot. He knew he had some loose change, his house key, and a handful of Ms. Dubois's cookies in his jacket. He was also still clutching two of the lockpicks from his set.

Jimmy shifted inside the dragging sack, moving so his head was nearer to the ground. He took a metal pick in each hand, brought them close together, and jabbed the ends through the burlap.

As soon as the picks pierced the sack, Jimmy slashed outward. His captor continued to pull the bag, and Jimmy tucked and rolled free through the torn opening.

Jimmy knew from the earlier slap that whoever took him was much, much stronger. He also knew that what happened in the shed was beyond a simple kidnapping. So, he didn't risk trying to fight whoever grabbed him.

Instead, he did what he did best: he ran. As soon as Jimmy was free, he got his feet under him and took off.

Unfortunately, a large oak tree directly in front of him blocked his flight. He hit it head-on, with a force strong enough to make him see stars and fall backward.

Jimmy groaned and rubbed his forehead.

"Lost little rabbit doesn't know its way."

Even in the darkness, Jimmy noticed the shadow falling over him. His vision clearing from the impact, he saw a tall, thin figure leaning down toward him.

He lashed out wildly with the sliver of metal.

His captor deftly dodged the swipes and erupted in high-pitched laughter. "Little rabbit has teeth!"

With a blur of movement, the lock picks were pulled from Jimmy's grasp.

"But we'll just pull them out."

Pain erupted in Jimmy's left hand.

"And put them somewhere safe."

Jimmy looked down in horror. The two lock picks pierced his hand, right through the palm.

He was too surprised to scream. He just stared at the wound for a moment, then leaned back to look up at his attacker.

Jimmy was not prepared for what he saw. He did scream, then—the scream of a wounded animal staring down a carnivorous grin.

His attacker laughed again, exposing far too many teeth for a human. "Easier to feed," he explained. The horrifying figure licked his thin lips and ran a finger along Jimmy's cheek.

His captor was impossibly thin, as if someone cinched gray, pallid flesh over a skeleton. The dimensions were also… wrong. He looked over six feet tall, but with thin arms that almost reached past his knees, and his hands were so long Jimmy thought each finger must contain an extra digit. Each finger also sported yellowing nails that came to sharp points. Despite his almost emaciated form, the creature radiated wiry strength and unnatural quickness. He wore no clothes, except for a threadbare pair of black britches held up on narrow hips by a rope; he also had a cracked, leather satchel slung over one shoulder.

But nothing caught Jimmy's attention more than the creature's face.

His head was a perfect circle, emphasized by a complete absence of hair. The creature's eyes were large and yellow with small, pinpoint pupils. His teeth reminded Jimmy of the unearthly fish that lived in the deepest depths of the ocean—there were too many of them, and they all resembled thin, razor sharp stalactites. A black tongue ran across the jagged maw, and he stared hungrily at Jimmy.

"Stay away from me," Jimmy warned, clutching his wounded hand.

The creature barked out a cruel laugh. "Stupid rabbit. You belong to Needlebone now."

Before Jimmy could blink, his captor kicked him in the face. He fell flat again and felt the creature grab one of his feet. Before he knew it, he was being dragged along once more.

Jimmy's heart raced, and a cold sweat trickled down from his forehead, mingling with the fresh blood from his hand.

The thing called Needlebone whistled and sang cheerfully as he pulled Jimmy deeper and deeper into the dark.

That's when Jimmy first started whispering to himself.

"Everything's going to be okay."

"Jack will come for me."

"He'll do the Look."

"And everything will be okay."

The Needlebone man whistled merrily in the darkness.

# CHAPTER SIX

The underworld left a lot to be desired.

When Jack stepped into the shed, he expected a fiery hellscape, a ghostly prison full of angry spirits dragging translucent chains, or even a more nightmarish version of the DMV. He found none of these. Instead, he stepped into a place scarcely dissimilar from what he left.

His boot landed on wet grass, and he looked up to see the same massive oaks he associated with Nebelwood Forest. Though the sun had been shining outside Mr. Porter's shed, Jack emerged into late evening dusk—light enough that Jack could see his immediate surroundings clearly.

The branches of ancient trees intertwined and wove a complex tapestry that reached to the heavens, but the trunks were widely spaced, and the ground was clear of growth. A dense fog around Jack's knees stretched as far as he could see. And though they were still in t-shirt weather outside the shed—the longest season in Mississippi, where jackets were typically required only two months out of the year—Jack felt a cold, sharp chill in the air of the Hinderwood.

He stood directly in front of a wooden door frame without a door. The frame struck him as rather unremarkable, until a sudden rush of wind and familiar blinding light flooded from the opening and illuminated the entire scene.

Jack instinctively raised his fists, but just as suddenly as it appeared, the rush of air died down and the light vanished. William Porter said the door acted like a beacon—Jack wondered how far away it would be visible.

He knocked twice on the frame to let the mortician know the signal worked.

Then, he scanned his surroundings for any sign of movement. Seeing none, he shrugged off his pack and pulled out his dark brown leather jacket, which had been made from thick buffalo hide and given to him by Cash about a year ago. Jack brought the jacket with him for its protective qualities, not because he expected any cold weather, but the chill in the air made him grateful for it. Ms. Dubois tailored it for Jack, so it fit him like a reassuring glove.

After he zipped the pack up again, he slipped it back onto his shoulder and scanned the area once more. Though he still didn't see any movement, he noticed a large, dark shape to his right.

Jack slipped his bat from its sheath, hefted the familiar weight, and started toward the bulky shadow. It looked to him like a copse of low trees, but Jack learned long ago to be careful and to verify.

As he approached, he was surprised to see something familiar: a house—William Porter's house, to be exact, though a more apocalyptic version. Nature had begun to reclaim it, as if in some long-defunct civilization. One massive oak grew directly through the center of the house, its branches and vines almost completely ensconcing the rest.

Jack stepped onto the porch and looked around. The door was partially covered by a branch, but it sat open, revealing absolute darkness within. Then Jack heard a soft, creaking noise above him, and he stepped back off the porch to look up at the roof of the house. A flutter of movement caught his eye near a partially shattered window, where he saw a faint light shining from inside.

Considering the otherwise shadowy interior of the derelict house, Jack contemplated the use of his own light—but a flashlight would just give away his position.

So, Jack slipped under the branch and into the house.

The showroom—or at least, what served as the showroom on the other side of the veil—was empty except for the oak tree and the occasional vine and branch snaking in from the outer wall. Wooden floorboards creaked softly as Jack crept across the empty space. In the back of the room, he discovered a stairway. Stopping, Jack untied his boots and slipped them off, leaving them on the floor with his pack. He slung the rifle back over his shoulder.

Holding the Heaven Breaker at the ready, Jack ascended the stairs, socked feet moving carefully and in silence. He surfaced in a hallway with three doors, and a faint glow spilled out from one that stood open. Jack placed his back to the wall, crouched low, and waited.

After counting to one hundred without anything stirring, Jack exhaled in a silent sigh and crept toward the doorway. Slowly craning his head around the frame, he peered inside.

A thin, half burnt-out candle rested in a tarnished silver holder on a small nightstand. Next to the nightstand, a neat pallet of quilts and pillows were stacked in a makeshift mattress. A dresser and a bookshelf flanked opposite walls. On the bookshelf, Jack noticed several books that looked worn and well-read.

He also saw a small, framed photo next to the candle on the nightstand. But when he stepped forward to examine it, he caught his reflection in the damaged windowpane and froze.

A boy in a fox mask stood directly behind him.

Jack turned and raised the bat defensively, narrowing his eyes at the strange person—a boy almost his own height, but wirier, and dressed in the same clothes as the night before.

Jack squinted, trying to see through the tiny eye-slits in the mask, to glimpse the real face behind it, but to no avail. All he saw were the lifeless, painted-plastic eyes of the fox.

"Who are you?"

The fox ghost said nothing. He cocked his head to the side, like an animal examining something strange.

Jack gritted his teeth angrily. "Did you take my brother?"

The fox ghost stared.

"Answer me!" Jack swung the bat. Not as hard as he could, but hard enough to get a cocky ghost's attention.

The fox ghost took a step backward, smoothly evading the bat and side-stepping behind Jack.

Jack recovered and pivoted sharply toward the spirit, sweeping his leg at the fox ghost's ankle in a wide, low arc. The masked spirit stepped backward again, but Jack spun and swung the bat in a violent uppercut. The fox ghost narrowly avoided the blow and caught his wrist as the Heaven Breaker sailed past. Jack lowered his shoulder and charged forward, sending them both into the window on the far side of the room.

The broken window cracked further but didn't shatter.

Before Jack could break his grip, the fox ghost reached out with his free hand and tapped the glass — not threateningly — almost as if trying to get his opponent's attention.

Jack paused.

The fox mask tilted slightly, indicating something on the other side of the window.

In spite of himself, Jack glanced outside. From his vantage point, he could see quite far. Though the trees went on for miles, he could make out narrow paths that branched throughout the misty forest. He also saw a nearby clearing.

His eyes fixed on the open space, or at least on what unfolded within it: several tall figures surrounded a much smaller, curled-up figure on the ground.

Jack turned sharply toward his foe—but he found himself alone in the dark room.

On his wrist, where the ghost grabbed him, Jack found a blue handprint. At first, he thought the ghost gripped him so hard that it left a bruise, but when he touched it, he winced. It felt more like a bad sunburn.

Jack shook off the pain. He had work to do.

He didn't bother searching for the fox ghost, hurrying straight downstairs and reclaiming his boots before grabbing his pack and rushing from the house. He ran through the forest, heading east toward the clearing. The thick mist and general darkness obscured any trail, so Jack darted around plenty of trees, though he moved in as straight a course as he could.

Before long, the trees thinned again, and Jack saw several dim lights hovering in the distance. He moved swiftly between the oaks, eventually coming to a spot that allowed him to stay hidden and view the scene before him. He wasn't sure what he was seeing, though.

It looked like Opossum Trot's Main Street, though another apocalyptic version like William Porter's house. A row of neglected brick buildings sported the same invasive oaks, and the street itself was cracked with vegetative shoots that forced their way through the crumbling pavement. One sapling sprouted out of a mailbox.

Strangely, the streetlights were still lit. The light-bulbs gave off a dim light that mostly emphasized the surrounding darkness but also cast a faint glow.

The bit of light illuminated the real focus of Jack's attention.

Four tall figures stood over a curled-up form, all wearing black-hooded sweatshirts and white gloves. Jack could only see their backs as they fixated on their prey. The hooded shape closest to it held a short-handled camp shovel.

The huddled figure whimpered. Jack stared hard and saw—both to his relief and disappointment—that it wasn't Jimmy, but a Black boy who looked big for his age. He couldn't have been more than seven or eight years old. He wore white rubber work boots and overalls.

He was crying.

Jack dropped his pack and his gun and strode into the clearing, knuckles white from gripping the bat and teeth fully clenched. He tried to make himself calm and focused, but—

The little boy was *crying*.

The lead figure swung the shovel at the boy, stopping just short of his head.

The boy flinched and sobbed.

"Ah! Two for flinching!" the figure yelled, raising the shovel high above his head.

"Stop."

The young boy looked up through his tears, and the four hoods all slowly turned to face Jack.

Beneath their cowls, they all wore masks made of burlap sacks. The sacks were painted to look like a variety of skulls, and none of the masks had holes cut for eyes. The figure with the shovel modeled a skull with its mouth painted open to reveal a circular maw of teeth.

It tilted its head curiously at Jack. "You must be new… Or just stupid."

Jack didn't waste time talking. He lunged forward and swung the bat. Because the figure was taller than him, Jack swung in a downward angle, aiming for its hip.

The bat whizzed harmlessly through the figure of the masked spirit.

"Ha, where'd you get your bat, chief?"

Without waiting for an answer, the masked figure slammed the shovel into the side of Jack's head.

Already off-balance from the missed shot, Jack fell to his knees.

The ghost in the skull mask brought the shovel down again. Jack tried to block the blow with the bat, but the shovel passed effortlessly through the oiled hardwood and hit him hard on the shoulder.

Jack fell flat. He saw the other hooded figures close in around him and sensed the leader raising the shovel again. Releasing his grip on the Heaven Breaker, Jack pushed himself up slightly and rolled —just as the shovel came down blade-first against the pavement where his face had been.

Before the leader could straighten, Jack tackled him at the waist and drove him to the ground, snapping a rabbit punch at its wrist. The shovel fell to the cracked pavement.

A gloved hand reached for Jack, but he pushed it aside and slammed his fist into the mask.

His knuckles connected with surprisingly brittle bones beneath the burlap.

When he pulled back to throw another punch, undeterred, a boot kicked him in the back of the head. Jack rolled and kicked out, but another boot hit him in the ribs.

Before he could get his bearings, the entire gang started stomping on him. Jack covered up and tried to collect himself, but the attack came from all directions. He tried to rise to a knee, but someone stomped hard on his lower back and sent him back down. When he managed to raise his head slightly, he saw the leader picking up the shovel again.

He also saw the little boy had gotten to his feet.

A kick to the face almost made Jack lose consciousness. He reached up to cover his head, bracing as he sensed the leader raise his shovel.

"Night-night, tough guy," he cackled.

"Leave… us… ALONE!"

Jack looked up in time to see the shovel yanked from the leader's hand.

The painted skeleton mask turned around, and where the boy stood a second before, there stood a giant—the largest man Jack had ever seen. He was close to seven-feet-tall, with over three hundred pounds of farm-boy muscle, and his hands looked like they could pop Jack's head like a water balloon.

One of those hands swung the shovel and cleaved through the waist of the leader. The shovel passed through, but unlike Jack's bat, it cut the hooded spirit in half. His legs and upper body fell into two separate piles.

Then, the hooded figure's body tried to turn itself inside out. As Jack watched, a crow's head popped through the space between the collar of its shirt and the burlap mask. It squawked angrily at Jack—then, a half-dozen crows erupted from the pants, sweatshirt, and hood, leaving the pile of clothes empty.

Jack turned back toward the gigantic man, who'd continued his assault on the rest of the gang. He tore through the remaining hoods like a rhino through a flock of flamingos, picking up one with a grinning skull mask and slamming it into the pavement. Gravel sprayed from the asphalt, and another murder of crows erupted from the clothes.

Jack rose gingerly to his feet as the man ripped the burlap sack from the last figure's head. A stream of black birds soared through the empty collar.

The large man panted heavily and stared at the sky. Jack looked up and saw the murder of crows hovering above them, forming up in a tight mass of feathered darkness.

In unison, they screamed and screeched before swirling away into the night.

For a moment, the pair just watched the birds depart in silence. Eventually, Jack broke the silence.

"Thanks. What's your name?" he asked, turning back toward the enormous man.

His eyes were defensive, like someone used to being hit, but Jack saw something else, too—something surprisingly hopeful.

A big hand extended toward Jack. "I'm Ben."

"Nice to meet you, Ben." When he shook Ben's hand, it completely swallowed his own.

Looking up at the man, Jack considered the two battles he'd already fought in the scant time he'd spent in the Hinderwood. He also recalled how easily the spirit named Ben tore through the crows.

With those thoughts in mind, Jack forced a small smile. "You want to hang out with me for a while?"

"Okay."

# INTERLUDE TWO:
## MS. DUBOIS

Though Renee Dubois had no kids of her own, she took care of children in various forms for generations. She spent a long life watching boys and girls grow into men and women, and, in many cases, playing a significant and positive role in their development. She was familiar with the challenges and trials of adolescence—perhaps more so than most parents. She knew when it was time to get involved and when space was needed. She knew how to walk the line between being firm but still communicating love and affection.

The Doe brothers had been through considerable challenges in their short lives, but Renee knew they were not unique in what they needed. They were exceptional children, in her opinion, but children first and foremost. By consistently displaying the right mix of love, patience, and trust, she gained their adoration and respect.

As such, she would not normally be overly concerned that the boys had not returned home following their Halloween night activities. But over the years, Renee also learned to trust her gut—and when she woke up the morning after Halloween, something felt wrong. She had a distinct feeling of worry for the boys, one that made her very uneasy.

Renee knew her unease likely had something to do with the picture she'd meant to show the Doe brothers. She kept it on her bedside table, so she would remember to show it to Jack and Jimmy first thing in the morning.

She wasn't alarmed by the contents of the picture. She was ninety-three years old, after all, and not easily surprised. Besides, William Porter had been a fixture in Opossum Trot for a long time, and she would know if he'd ever hurt anyone, especially a child.

But something felt odd, and she wished she would have shown the photo to the boys—just as she suspected she should have shown the boys the contents of the manila folder gathering dust in her nightstand. She'd put certain things off for too long, and that morning, she feared it might have gotten too late to stop whatever bad was clearly coming.

So, that morning, after waiting for the boys for one last hour, Renee rose from her breakfast of oatmeal with a sprinkle of cinnamon and sliced banana, and she put on one of her going-into-town dresses. She didn't have time for her hair, so she opted for a sensible blue, felt hat with a yellow ribbon in the band.

When she was satisfied with her appearance, she gathered her effects into her large leather purse. Then, after thinking for a long moment, she also gathered both the photo and the manila folder from her nightstand. All things collected, she got into her old Buick LeSabre and backed out the long dirt road that served as her driveway.

She knew the Doe Brothers planned on going to the mortician's. But she thought it best to check the more usual spots first. She overheard the brothers say they wanted to borrow supplies from Buford and Cash—so Renee decided she would start there.

Δ

Renee stepped out of her car in front of the old farmhouse.

"Well, this is a treat," said Cash, with a bright smile.

"Morning, Renee," Buford chimed in. "We still got some biscuits and deer sausage from breakfast. Can I tempt you?"

"You haven't managed to yet," said Renee with a wry smile.

"Not for lack of trying," Buford replied with a grin of his own.

"Well, what can we do for you this morning, Renee?" asked Cash. "You know you oughtn't be getting out like this just to see us."

"That's enough of that talk now," Renee said with a hint of sharpness. "I'm not dead yet, and I won't be lectured by you two. I'm looking for Jack and Jimmy. Have they been by today?"

Over the years, Renee developed quite the affinity for reading children's body language. She could spot even the most subtle signs of guilt in a child, if she'd watched them grow up.

She'd gotten the most practice with the particular boys in front of her.

Despite Buford and Cash's advanced ages, they were far from experts at subtlety. When Cash's nostrils flared slightly and Buford looked up at the ceiling fan that hummed away on the porch, Renee knew what it meant.

"What did you boys do?" she asked, her tone lowering in a warning.

"Promise you won't get mad," said Buford, warily.

Renee Dubois said nothing out loud, but her answer came through clearly to the two old men, who shrank sheepishly in anticipation of a sure-fire chewing out.

They shared a look, then Cash pointed at his friend and blurted out, "Buford talked to Jack earlier today!"

"You dirty—!" started Buford incredulously, stopping when Renee furrowed her brow and raised a warning finger. The old man in the denim jacket relented. "He came by here earlier. Didn't stay though, he was pretty wound up. Said he had to take care of something important."

"Was Jimmy with him?"

"No, just him. I got the sense it had to do with the younger one, though," said Buford, staring at his boots.

"What else?"

"What do you mean, what else?"

"What else did you do?" Renee's brow remained furrowed.

"Why does there have to be something else?" he asked, indignantly.

Renee looked at Cash.

Cash started to open his mouth to reply, but Buford punched his shoulder.

"Okay, dang it! So much for loyalty." Buford glared at Cash, then looked back to Renee. "He *may* have taken a rifle and some ammo with him."

Renee was not a woman easily surprised or ruffled. During her ninety-three years in the town of Opossum Trot, she came across some mind-blowingly asinine situations. She would have said that man's capacity for stupidity was immense, as she felt she had experienced first-hand the farthest reaches on that scale. She also would have sworn that these two particular men could not have surprised her anymore.

She realized she had been wrong on both counts.

She opened her mouth, then closed it again. She pointed at Buford, started to say something, stopped, then pointed at Cash. She seemed to reconsider that as well.

Finally, she took a deep breath and said, "You two might be the dumbest men I've ever met, and at my age, that should give you some pause."

"What'd I do?!" Cash asked with exasperation.

Buford said, "Oh, come on Renee! They ain't children, when we were their age—"

"If you think you two are suitable role models, that only makes my point!" she said angrily, breathing heavily—she hadn't been this worked up in a while. An increasingly familiar tightness rose in her chest, and though she did her best to ignore it, she saw the boys noticing.

"Renee?" said Buford, sounding very concerned.

"Why don't you take a seat for a spell?" Cash took a step toward her, but she held up a hand.

"I've got to find my boys." Renee turned and started back toward her car.

Buford and Cash shared a knowing but concerned look. There was no sense arguing.

Then, Buford remembered something and perked up. "If it makes you feel better, that rifle's only a bolt action!"

Renee stuck her head out the window of her silver Buick LeSabre and stared at the overgrown children—at the aging boys she loved with all her heart, who frustrated her to no apparent end.

"Idiots." Renee shook her head, rolled up her window, and drove toward town.

# CHAPTER SEVEN

Once they felt confident nothing else would try to kill them for the time being, Jack and Ben made their way together through the woods. Ben told Jack they needed to leave Main Street—he said only monsters used the main roads.

Instead, they walked down a cobblestone path that ran through the forest. While they traveled, Jack told Ben about Jimmy. Jack was laconic by nature, but he found it easy to talk with Ben. He spoke about his brother's love of Japanese cartoons, mystery novels, and junk food—despite his thin frame and gifted running speed. He told Ben about New Orleans, coming to Opossum Trot, and how Jimmy came to be in the Hinderwood.

When he described the thin, bony arm that grabbed his brother, the older man nodded in recognition.

"You know who took Jimmy?" Jack asked, hoping.

"Not sure. But it could be the Needlebone Man," Ben replied, in his increasingly-familiar deep baritone.

"Needlebone Man?"

"He's a monster. I've heard about him. He's real skinny like a skeleton, but tough." Ben paused. "And he can change himself."

"Change himself?"

"Yeah, he can be different people. And I heard he takes children."

"Why?" Jack asked, afraid of the answer.

"For food. But he doesn't just eat 'em. He makes them last real long."

"What do you mean?"

"He preserves them. Like with pig lips." Ben looked at Jack. "…you like pig lips?"

"They're okay." Jack tried them when he first moved to Opossum Trot. As he walked, he tried not to think about the process of pickling a *person*—especially not Jimmy.

He looked back at Ben. "Do you know where I can find the Needlebone Man?"

Ben considered this. "I've never seen him before. Just heard stories." Ben seemed like he was trying to remember something. "I think I heard he takes them to some place near the Edge."

"The Edge?"

"Edge of all this." Ben gestured to their surroundings. "Nothing's past the Edge."

"How do I get there?"

"Just go west till there ain't nothing else. Going that way now."

Jack thought on this. A monster who preserved and ate people kidnapped his brother, and it was taking him to the edge of Hell.

However, at least Jack had a lead—one that was easy enough to run down, assuming he could avoid getting into fights with every messed-up spirit in the woods. He thought about the fox ghost and the crows in the skeleton masks.

"Is everyone here a monster?" he asked.

The towering man in the overalls stopped walking.

Jack wasn't expecting the sudden stop, and he kept going for a few steps before skidding to a halt.

When he turned back, he raised an eyebrow in surprise. The massive man in the overalls was gone. In his place stood the stocky little boy who'd been crying under the thumb of the crows. Young Ben looked utterly crestfallen. His brow furrowed sadly, and his lower lip practically trembled.

"I'm not a monster…"

"I'm sorry," Jack said, realizing his mistake. "I wasn't talking about you, Ben. I just meant I've hardly been here two hours, and I've already fought monsters twice."

"I'm good though, right?" Ben asked, looking at his feet. He was still wearing a smaller version of his overalls, but the white rubber boots had vanished. He stood in bare feet.

"You're great, Ben. I promise. Hey, can I ask you another question?"

"Sure." Ben brightened and started walking once more. As he continued down the path, Jack saw his companion quickly revert to his larger, adult form.

"Why are you here?" Jack looked around at the thick mist and the dense, dark forest. "Doesn't seem like… your kind of place."

"I'm waiting for my brother."

"Seriously?"

"Yeah."

Jack waited, but Ben didn't say anything else. They walked in silence for a while.

"Why are there some… creatures, like the crows and the Needlebone Man, but then there's guys like you here?" Jack asked.

"Just like it was on the other side," Ben shrugged. "Some people just getting by, others taking advantage. But this place makes it easier to tell 'em apart."

"Yeah?"

"Needlebone, those crows—they used to be people. That's why you could still hit them with your fists but not that bat."

"What do you mean?"

"The bat's from a world they don't remember. They used to be made of flesh, though. Hard to forget that."

"They really used to be human?"

"Yeah. But the longer you spend here, feeding on others, the more it changes you."

Jack thought for a while, then eventually asked, "You know anyone that wanders around in a fox mask?"

"Fox mask?" Ben bunched his eyebrows. "No. Don't know anyone like that. Why?"

"Just someone I keep running into."

Δ

Jack and Ben walked a long time. After a while, the eldest Doe brother saw a brief, brilliant flash in the sky coming from the direction of the gate. The sight reassured him—the mortician was keeping up his end of the deal.

He found he enjoyed Ben's company. Ben was soft spoken and amiable, if still a little childlike even in his adult form. He learned that Ben lived in Opossum Trot for most of his life—and they actually had even more than that in common. Ben was an orphan too, primarily raised by his older brother. They even knew some of the same people. Ben could remember Ms. Dubois's reading time from when he was a little boy.

Though Jack wanted to know how Ben died, it seemed impolite to ask. He figured a person's death could be a personal topic. But he sensed that his new friend had been in the Hinderwood for a while.

Jack made sure to be mindful of the time, checking the timer William Porter gave him while they walked along the path. According to the ticking numbers, he'd been in the Hinderwood for almost five hours—he still had more than an entire day to find Jimmy. Hopefully, his brother could hold out long enough for him to get them both back through the shed.

"So, your brother's nice?" Ben asked, drawing him out of his musings.

"He's a good kid. Not many people who grew up like we did could be so happy."

"You looked out for him?"

"Yeah. He's too gentle for stuff like this."

"My brother and I looked out for each other a lot. We had to," Ben said.

"Yeah."

"I thought you were him, at first. When those crows were scaring me."

"Why were they doing that?" Jack asked.

"I get lonely sometimes, and sad. It's like the monsters can tell, and they come for you." When he said so, Ben once again reverted to his younger form. Before Jack could say anything to make him feel better, the stocky child in the overalls gestured to something on the road ahead.

Jack looked forward and saw the cobblestone path growing narrow and leading to a dark hollow of trees. The oaks lining the path arched together across the slim trail to create a kind of tunnel. Many of the trees had strange writing carved into their ancient bark.

The eldest Doe brother's attention fixed on the path itself, however—or rather, on what stood in its way. Somehow, Jack hadn't noticed until Ben pointed it out, but a ten-foot-tall barrier of brilliant white stone crossed over the road in front of them.

"That's the way to the Memory Forest," said Young Ben, staring up at the towering barrier.

"What is it?"

"Things from your past come looking for you in there," Ben explained.

"That should be interesting," Jack muttered.

He stepped back until he was far enough to get a running start, then he bolted toward the wall. At the last moment, Jack leapt into the air and reached for the top of the stone barrier—but his hands didn't come within four feet of the stone lip.

Unphased, he landed roughly and tried again. He still didn't come close to the top.

Then, he slipped off his backpack and unfastened the closure, rummaging through the bag.

"I know I packed it," he muttered. "Here we go."

Jack held up a length of strong, black cord attached to a heavy-looking, four-pronged metal head.

Young Ben shrugged.

Jack looked up at the wall, swinging the barbed end of the grappling hook in a whirring arc at his side. When he'd built enough momentum, Jack released the cord and let the hooked rope fly up toward the top of the wall.

Though the wall had flat edges, as the hook settled on the corner of one, the barrier suddenly shifted, curving. Unable to find purchase, the grappling hook slid off the wall and fell to the ground in front of Jack.

"Was it supposed to do that?" Ben asked.

Jack didn't answer, retrieving the tool and sliding it back into his bag. Instead of shrugging the pack over his shoulder, however, he left it on the ground and walked toward the wall.

The forest trees looked dense along each side of the stone fence, but Jack thought he and Ben could probably wedge through them if they tried. Stepping off the path, he tried to peer around the corner to get a better look.

To his surprise, the wall suddenly extended farther from the path than he previously thought. He took a couple more steps, but the wall continued to expand to meet him. He never actually saw the white barrier move, but no matter how hard he tried, he couldn't seem to reach the edge. Eventually, he sighed and returned to the cobblestone path.

Young Ben scratched his head. "That was weird."

"What isn't, here," Jack said with mild irritation, rubbing his chin thoughtfully. After a moment, he turned to his companion. "Ben, I'm going to need your help getting over the wall."

Ben offered a small smile and tentatively walked up to the wall. When he stood within arm's reach, he spread his feet slightly, cupped his hands together in front of him, and braced his shoulders. He nodded at Jack.

"Okay, I'm ready," said the little boy, sounding nervous.

Jack blinked at Ben, who—in his current form—was even shorter than Jimmy. Judging by the wall's height, Jack would need six feet of clearance to reach the top.

He politely cleared his throat. "Here's the deal, Ben. You're probably going to need to get big again."

"Big?" asked Young Ben.

"Yeah, like when you beat up those crows."

"But… *you* saved me from those crows," said the stocky boy, looking mildly confused but hesitant to seem disagreeable.

Jack didn't reply right away. He looked at Ben and thought of how his new friend shifted back and forth from a small, timid boy to a behemoth, trying to recall the moments of change and what seemed to trigger them.

After some deliberation, he knelt down so that he and Ben were eye to eye.

"I haven't been in this place long, but it seems to feed on fears, and maybe insecurities. I think you let this place get in your head, and you forget how strong you are."

"It's scary here, though," said Ben, softly.

"I know. But when you saw me in trouble with those crows, you forgot about all that and *you* saved *me*."

"I did…?"

"You did. You're strong, Ben. You're also the biggest guy I've ever met," Jack said earnestly.

"I am?"

"See for yourself."

Adult Ben looked down in surprise, seeming to see himself at his full size for the first time. His eyes widened, and he held up hands that looked large enough to twist rebar.

"Strong people should help others. Right?" said Jack.

With a quiet but confident voice, Ben said, "I can help."

Before Jack could say anything else, his friend reached down and grasped him under his arms. With startling speed, he half-lifted, half-tossed the eldest Doe brother toward the top of the wall. Jack was surprised, but he managed to reach a hand out for the edge of the barrier.

Though he half-expected the wall to change again, to his relief, his hand caught the top of the strange fence, and he was able to pull himself up and sit on top of the wall. He took a breath and ran his hand through his hair.

"Well, I guess that worked. Thanks."

Ben smiled and gathered Jack's bag and rifle, tossing up the supplies.

The eldest Doe brother caught his belongings and carefully sat them on top of the wall beside him. That accomplished, he looked down at Ben and scratched his head thoughtfully.

"Let's see… I can probably tie the grappling hook rope to something on the other side, and you can climb—" He stopped when he saw Ben shaking his head. "What's wrong?" he asked.

"I can't go in there," said Ben.

"Why?"

"It's bad for me in there." Ben nodded at the dense hollow of trees on the other side. "Stuff from the past scares me." He seemed embarrassed, but also firm.

"I understand," said Jack. Then, looking around, he asked, "Is there another way around?"

"I don't think so."

"You sure you can't come with me? Maybe together we can—"

But Ben was already shaking his head. "I'd better not. Besides, I need to get back, in case my brother shows up."

Jack stared into his companion's kind eyes. "Ben?"

"Yeah?"

"Have you thought about… moving on? Not waiting around here anymore?"

"I can't go without my brother," said Ben, as if it was the most obvious thing in the world.

And in a way, it was—and Jack felt foolish.

"Thanks for walking with me, Ben."

"It's nice to have company. I hope you find Jimmy."

"Me too. See you around."

With that, he reached down to shake hands with his new friend, and they each turned and went their separate ways: Ben leaving to wait for his older brother, and Jack lowering himself down into the Memory Forest.

# INTERLUDE THREE: JIMMY

Jimmy wasn't sure how long the Needlebone Man dragged him.

In the meantime, he managed to pull the lock-picks from his palm and wrap his wound tightly with a strip he tore from his shirt. His hand stung, but eventually, it gave way to a painful throb—an unpleasant but manageable pain, as long as he kept his arm from dangling.

The Needlebone Man didn't seem to mind Jimmy's activities, as long as he didn't resist the dragging.

After what felt like hours, he passed out.

When he awoke, he was lying flat on his back, and he could feel something tight around his leg. Raising his head, he saw a rusty manacle encircling his ankle just above his foot. A chain affixed to the manacle wrapped and locked around a streetlight, of all things.

Jimmy didn't understand the strange world he'd been taken into, but public infrastructure seemed out of place.

After scanning his immediate vicinity, he felt still more surprise to see a run-down town. He lay in the middle of a road with buildings on both sides. He even saw a handful of vehicles haphazardly parked in the road and on the sidewalk.

The ghostly town looked on its last legs, though, with nature fighting its way back into control. Thick, green ivy climbed up the walls of all the buildings, and oak trees—like the one that blocked Jimmy's escape from the sack—grew through the concrete and asphalt. He noticed that the tires on all the cars were flat, and vegetation peeked out from under most of the hoods.

Movement caught his eye: a shudder in the black interior of one of the closest buildings. Its door hung open on rusted hinges.

Jimmy strained to peer closer, to make out whatever moved in the dark.

Suddenly, two glowing eyes appeared in the doorway, standing out against the darkness of the unlit shop.

Jimmy's breath caught in his throat, but before he could react, another pair of eyes opened, quickly followed by three more sets. Then, the front window of the shop also filled with pale, yellow eyes—all watching Jimmy hungrily.

A small, pale hand like a toddler's pressed its palm against the dusty glass, longingly.

Jimmy opened his mouth to scream.

"Don't worry, little rabbit. The empty ones won't feast on what belongs to Needlebone."

The Needlebone Man crouched low at Jimmy's feet like an oversized but emaciated frog. He grinned at the youngest Doe brother with far too many thin, pointed teeth.

Jimmy hadn't noticed the creature approach. Had he been there the whole time, just out of sight? "Why are you doing this?" Jimmy asked.

"You'll feed Needlebone for a long time. Have to get you home first, though, to preserve you nice and proper."

"Where are we?" Jimmy nodded at his dismal surroundings.

Needlebone grinned wickedly and spread his arms wide, like a ringmaster at a demented circus.

"Welcome to Heaven, little rabbit!"

"Heaven?"

"No divine choruses, I fear; we ate all the angels. Tasted like pigeon."

When they lived on their own, before Opossum Trot, Jimmy sometimes played in City Park while Jack worked. One day, he'd been reading a comic book at the Peristyle, leaning against one of the stone lions, when a shadow passed over him.

He looked up to see a woman smiling at him. She wore sweatpants and a long coat, despite the summer heat. Her hair was unkempt and tangled. And something was wrong with her smile—it was too tight and strangely aggressive.

She held a hand with chipped nail polish out toward Jimmy.

"Come along, dear."

"Uh, what?"

"It's time to go home. Let's get going, you can come play some other time," she said, in a sing-song voice.

"I think you've got the wrong kid," Jimmy said, confused.

"None of that, dear." Before he realized what was happening, the woman grabbed his hand and began pulling him away from the lion statue.

"Hey! Let go!" Jimmy yelled and tried to pull free, but she gripped his hand tighter and kept pulling him.

"We have to get home for dinner!" she exclaimed loudly. The manic smile never faltered.

"Hey!"

The next thing Jimmy knew, his older brother was there, pulling the woman's hand off his wrist. Once he was free from the woman's grasp, Jack pushed him away from her outstretched arms, silently telling him to get to safety.

Jimmy ran. As he escaped, he could hear Jack telling the now-sobbing woman that she was mistaken.

Jack met him later at their campsite. He told Jimmy the woman wasn't bad—she was just crazy.

Jimmy felt pretty sure Needlebone was bad. But he had the same wide-eyed, manic look as the woman in the park when she insisted it was time for Jimmy to go home with her.

So, Jimmy knew he had to be careful.

"Is Needlebone your name?"

"Name? No names here, little rabbit. Just words for predators and prey." The ghoul man flashed his stiletto teeth. "Needlebone is greatest predator of all. King of predators."

"So, there are others here like me?" Jimmy asked. "Are normal people prey?"

Needlebone opened his mouth to answer, but then, he suddenly froze. His already-enormous eyes widened.

Jimmy started to ask what was going on, but the thin monster shot forward and covered his mouth with a bony hand. The youngest Doe brother glanced toward the nearby building and saw the short, dark figures with the glowing eyes receding quickly into the darkness.

Then Jimmy heard the breathing.

It sounded like someone exhaling softly into an unseen but high-powered microphone. The sound came from every direction. It wasn't loud, exactly, but it was deliberate, and something about the noise gripped Jimmy's stomach in terror.

Needlebone produced a small key from the pocket of his threadbare pants and began fumbling with the lock and chain wrapped around the streetlamp. "We must leave! The Pursuer approaches."

"The Pursuer?" Jimmy asked, staring at the chain falling free from the lock.

"Quiet, rabbit! We must flee!"

Jimmy saw a tall, dark shape emerge from the thick fog at the opposite end of the street. Needlebone saw it too and shuddered. He tried to jerk Jimmy to his feet, but the youngest Doe resisted.

"You have to get this off my leg," he said, gesturing to the manacle that still encircled his ankle.

Needlebone stared at Jimmy suspiciously. He started to say something, but then the all-encompassing breathing began again.

He snarled, "If you try to escape me, I'll take your feet and make you crawl!" Then, he inserted the key into a slot on the manacle and twisted. The restraint fell free, and Needlebone tucked it, the lock, and the chain back into his satchel.

"Now—" Needlebone began, but before he could finish his thought, Jimmy punched him in the groin and bolted down the street as fast as he could.

Jimmy heard Needlebone cursing furiously behind him, but he didn't hear any sounds of pursuit. He didn't turn to check; he just kept running.

The Needlebone Man clearly feared this new monster, so Jimmy ran in its general direction before darting away down a side street.

Jimmy didn't let himself turn back. He forced his thoughts away from the Needlebone Man, and he pushed aside any concerns over this new, potentially worse creature. He kept his breathing level and simply did what he did best.

He ran.

Δ

The youngest Doe brother ran longer than he'd ever run, keeping at least a jogging pace for hours. He stopped only briefly to eat some of Ms. Dubois's cookies and drink some dark, icy water running from a pipe into a side street. As he refreshed himself, he kept close watch for Needlebone and for the larger, dark shape the ghoul called "The Pursuer."

He also took a moment to examine the wound in his palm, which had turned red around the edges. His skin was beginning to swell. Shuddering, he rewrapped his hand.

Though he started to run again, he realized quickly that he needed to let his energy build up first.

He decided to take shelter in a nearby building.

Like every structure he'd seen since arriving at that place, the building fought a losing battle against decay and a vengeful Mother Nature. To move forward, Jimmy had to step over a branch as thick as an elephant's leg that grew across the linoleum floor.

Jimmy couldn't tell if the building had been a school, a hospital, or something alien, whose intended purposes he couldn't understand. Whatever the place was, it had many long hallways and an abundance of empty rooms. It seemed like a good place to hide until he could figure out a way to get back home. His footsteps echoed loudly as he walked through the long, empty hallways.

Jimmy stopped in front of a pair of double doors with a single window slit—but the glass was too dirty for him to see through it. When he looked both directions down the hallway, he saw no sign of movement.

Shrugging, Jimmy opened the door.

To his surprise, he found an empty auditorium with rows of sagging and broken seats. The velvet cushions were faded and torn, and a lot of the stuffing had been pulled free as if by an animal. A crimson curtain with golden tassels hung from the rafters and obscured the main stage.

He walked down the center aisle. As he got closer to the stage, he noticed a small set of stairs leading up to the performance area. Jimmy wasn't sure why, but he ascended the stairs. The acoustics in the auditorium were phenomenal. Every beat of Jimmy's sneakers reverberated through the dilapidated theater.

The curtain was still in good condition, despite the decay everywhere else. The brilliant red fabric transfixed him, shining boldly like a Spartan's cloak. Jimmy noticed a slight part in the middle and a pulley system that would open and close the curtain. When he put his ear to the fabric, he heard faint music on the other side.

Jimmy reached for the curtain.

"You know, curiosity turns many into involuntary denizens of this place."

Jimmy whirled around in terror, expecting to see Needlebone lunging for him. But there was no sign of him, and the speaker's voice was not the medley of gleeful rasping that Jimmy associated with his former captor.

The new voice was rich and deep and dripped with disdain from the back of the auditorium.

A man sat in one of the damaged chairs. He was nicely dressed—weirdly so, considering his surroundings. He wore a gray three-piece suit with a white shirt and a black tie. He also sported a pair of white opera gloves, and a black handkerchief emerged partially from the breast pocket of his suit jacket.

His neat appearance matched his clothes. His short, black hair parted sharply on the right side. His face had a narrow, angular quality, with high cheekbones and a defined jaw. He had a slim physique, but with the healthy, athletic leanness of a mountain lion, as opposed to the skeletal thinness of the Needlebone Man.

As Jimmy sized him up, the man removed his handkerchief and wiped it across his pale mouth. Then, he flicked the black cloth into the aisle, like he was shaking the sand off a beach towel. Something wet and dark splattered onto the floor.

"Who are you?" Jimmy asked.

Even from a distance, he could see the man in the gray suit roll his eyes. "Would you find it audacious, if an insect approached you and demanded your name?"

"Like a talking grasshopper?"

The well-dressed figure stared at Jimmy for several moments before eventually sighing. "Seeing oneself accurately is rare, indeed."

Jimmy raised a quizzical eyebrow. "What are you talking—"

Jimmy stopped short when the air between him and the man seemed to shimmer.

Then, the man in the gray suit suddenly stood with him on the stage. His pale, well-manicured hand clenched Jimmy's jaw so tightly, it felt like the bottom of his skull would shatter.

The man took three rapid steps forward, pushing Jimmy off his balance. The youngest Doe brother flailed his arms and legs in a vain attempt to keep from falling, but to his horror, before he could slump to the ground, the man in the gray suit—with no apparent effort—lifted him wholly off the ground.

The man in the suit spoke softly through clenched teeth. "I do not repeat myself. Nor do I converse casually, particularly not with vermin like yourself. Therefore, think carefully before you speak to me!" Jimmy saw an odd flash of crimson when the man's mouth opened, and he got a whiff of something rancid and dead.

Jimmy gasped and gurgled, trying desperately to fill his lungs. He tore at the hand holding his jaw, but it was like trying to scrape through granite. He managed to aim a kick at the man's solar plexus, like Jack taught him, but his attacker didn't even flinch, and his foot screamed in pain as if he'd kicked a brick wall.

The corners of his vision began to darken, but the impossible grip suddenly loosened, and Jimmy fell hard to the floor of the stage. His chest heaved as he tried to bring his breathing back to normal.

Once he got a good breath, he rolled into a defensive stance and scanned the room for his adversary.

To his surprise, the man in the gray suit once again sat in the chair at the back of the auditorium. His gloved hands folded neatly in his lap, and he stared at Jimmy with a mixture of disdain and mild amusement. "Now, how does a living boy find himself here?"

"I was just looking for somewhere safe to rest."

"I am unconcerned as to how you found yourself in this *building*." The man sighed impatiently and inspected his gloves. "I am interested in how you came to be wandering around the fields of the dead and forgotten. How did Needlebone come to claim your spirit?"

Jimmy just stared at him. He was hesitant to ask any more questions, for fear of setting the man off again.

His confusion must have registered clearly enough. The gray-suited man tapped his own ankle and nodded slightly.

Jimmy looked down, then pulled up the left leg of his jeans. Where the manacle earlier circled his leg, he found a small scar. He didn't know how he'd scarred already, after only wearing the chain for such a short time—but that would be just another item on a growing list of strange things he didn't understand about his present circumstances.

He looked closer at the scar. What he'd initially taken for an X was actually what looked like a bone crossed over a large darning needle.

"You're fortunate, in a way. Many lesser threats will avoid you, for fear of him. Now, how did you get here?"

"I was pulled through a glowing utility shed."

At this, the man bristled slightly. The air shimmered again, and instantly, he stood on the stage in front of Jimmy. The youngest Doe brother flinched, but the white gloves didn't reach for his throat. Instead, the man wearing them regarded him curiously.

"The witch doctor opened the gate?" he asked with apparent surprise.

"No," said Jimmy, wondering if he meant William Porter. "My brother and I did... for a Halloween... thing." His voice fizzled out lamely, as he realized his inability to articulate his recent activities.

With a hiss of air, the strange man disappeared.

But Jimmy had only one moment to consider using the opportunity to retreat, before the man in the gray suit reappeared exactly where he'd been.

"Foolish to hope it remained open, but worth investigating, nevertheless. The old shaman has managed to surprise me." He regarded the youngest Doe brother with renewed interest. "You mentioned a brother. Is he here, as well?"

"I don't know."

The man raised an eyebrow. There was something intense and threatening about the expression, and Jimmy hurried to explain.

"He wasn't taken like I was, but he'll come for me."

The neatly dressed man stared at Jimmy for a long moment, probing for any signs of dishonesty. After a while, apparently satisfied, he replied, "How noble of him," in a voice that clearly indicated he found nothing gallant at all in Jack's pursuit of his younger brother.

Jimmy said nothing.

The man stared out at the empty auditorium, suddenly lost in thought.

Jimmy thought about running, but only for a moment. The strange character could clearly teleport, or at least move so quickly he was essentially teleporting—what use would there be in trying to outrun him? So, Jimmy waited, trying to look respectful but not fearful.

"I think I will allow you to leave, young man," said the stern, polished voice.

Jimmy looked up in some surprise. "I can go?"

"Oh, yes. I believe you are of infinite more use to me alive."

"…Thank you…"

Jimmy slowly backed away from the man.

When he reached the stairs, he turned and tried not to look nervous as he walked away. He didn't want to trigger the man's wrath, if he was serious about letting him go.

When he'd made it halfway to the door, the stranger spoke again. "Oh, and young man—"

Jimmy flinched. "Yes, sir?" He turned around, bracing himself.

"Be careful out there."

Here, the man grinned, and it took every ounce of self-control Jimmy had not to gasp.

The man's teeth were the color of watered-down red paint, as if they'd been marinating in blood. And perhaps they had—because Jimmy saw several streams of red liquid trickling from the roots of his teeth.

Jimmy left as quickly as possible.

The stranger's humorless chuckles followed him for some time.

# CHAPTER EIGHT

Jack passed through the tight hollow of trees and came out on the other side, emerging onto a new cobblestone path that cut through the forest. He half-expected some new monster, based on what Ben said, but found only more trees and fog.

Once he felt confident that nothing would jump out at him, Jack decided to check the timepiece again. What he saw made him want to groan.

More than six hours had passed since he left William Porter's.

Jack forced himself to think on the bright side—he did have a good idea of where this Needlebone guy would go.

Besides, Jimmy must have known Jack would follow him. And his little brother could tough it out, if he knew Jack would be on his way.

Jack continued down the path for several miles, only pausing once, when he noticed the sky light up to the East. He turned toward the illumination, a stunning beam clearly visible even from where he stood. To Jack, it resembled a luminescent pillar reaching into the heavens.

As he stared at the light, he felt his pulse quicken and his heart race. Though Jack recognized the slow-building panic he associated with the Nightmare, he didn't look away. He held his gaze on the light and gritted his teeth against the rising terror.

Jimmy and Ms. Dubois would have been surprised to learn that Jack was sometimes lucid during the bad dream. In those moments, he'd become consciously aware of his own slumber—but despite the horror of the Nightmare, he didn't wake himself. He tried to ride it out, to weather the storm of fear without being overcome.

It never worked.

When Jack started to shake involuntarily, he looked away and took deep breaths until the panic subsided. When he calmed down, he looked back in the direction of the beam and saw that it had vanished once again.

He nodded in gratitude to William Porter and kept walking.

Eventually, he stopped for a short rest to munch on one of Buford and Cash's MREs. He'd grabbed four without paying much attention, and the options he'd inadvertently chosen disappointed him. He'd brought two teriyaki beef, a spaghetti, and a veggie burger. He settled on a teriyaki beef and tried to make the best of it, only giving himself ten minutes to eat and to rest.

Before leaving, he knelt and said a quick prayer—not for himself or even for Jimmy, but because he felt guilty about not telling Ms. Dubois what happened. He hated lying to her, and he knew she must have been worried. So, as a way of making it up to her, he offered a few quick but sincere words.

Then, Jack moved on.

Eventually, he noticed the landscape changing. The fog and the dim half-light remained, but the terrain slowly shifted. The dense trees grew more distant from one another, and large, green, moss-covered swaths carpeted the ground between the oaks. Pools of water rippled and splashed suddenly whenever Jack passed, as if small creatures were scurrying to the safety of murky depths. The path itself also changed—the cobblestone road gave way to a simple dirt trail, with small side trails branching off the main road.

Jack ignored these entirely and continued his pursuit.

As Jack traveled through the woods, he noticed himself becoming more introspective than usual. His thoughts turned to New Orleans and to Ms. Dubois—but mostly to his brother.

Fresh waves of guilt for the Halloween night debacle washed over him. He replayed the events at William Porter's shed over and over in his mind, out-lining all the ways he could have stopped Needlebone from taking Jimmy. Whether he lingered in that moment because of the Memory Forest or not, Jack was no stranger to prolonged guilt trips—he'd expected something more foreboding based on Ben's warnings.

But after some time, Jack noticed a soft pitter-patter echoing from behind, a faint but persistent noise on either side of the trail. However, when he stopped walking, the woods went silent again.

Jack sighed and unslung the rifle from his shoulder, racking a round into the chamber and checking the safety. When he started moving again, instead of slinging the gun back over his shoulder, Jack held it across his body—such that the stock nestled loosely in his right shoulder and the barrel pointed at the ground on his opposite side. He held the handle firmly in his right hand, and he kept his left hand on the wooden foregrip.

As he walked, he took long, steady breaths, inhaling deeply through his nostrils and exhaling evenly through his mouth. He cleared his mind and focused on his senses. His eyes scanned ahead and to the side for any sudden movements; his ears listened carefully for the faintest sounds of approach.

Jack could hear the soft crunch of light footsteps creeping closer, but he made no move to turn around. He waited patiently.

Finally, he heard a soft crunch followed by a quiet thud—the sound of someone stepping from a forest floor littered with twigs and acorns onto a dusty trail.

Jack whirled around, sending up a cloud of dust as he pivoted in a sharp 180-degree turn and brought the rifle to bear. He didn't fire, but he readied himself, his finger familiar with the weight of the trigger. The barrel didn't move, and the sights didn't shake even slightly on his target.

The fox mask's painted eyes stared at Jack. The lean specter still wore the olive-green jacket and work boots, but he'd acquired a small leather backpack since their last meeting. The strange figure's hands were empty, and he made no move to attack Jack.

He did cock his head slightly, as if asking the eldest Doe brother a question.

After a tense moment, Jack removed his finger from the trigger, but he did not lower the rifle. "What do you want?"

The fox boy stared at him for a long time without saying anything.

"I asked you a question! What do you want? Why are you following me?"

The ghost in the mask started to raise his right hand.

Jack tensed and returned his finger to the trigger.

The ghost noticed and paused. He slowly displayed an open, empty palm—reassuringly. Once Jack seemed satisfied, he raised his hand again, pointing a finger at Jack.

The eldest Doe brother watched in confusion.

Then, he raised his finger to the mask, tapping his forehead deliberately three times.

Jack raised an eyebrow. "What?"

The fox ghost sighed in mild irritation. The mask shook back and forth slightly with disapproval. He started to raise his hand again—but paused. Instead of pointing again, he displayed a finger gun, aiming it first to Jack's left, then his right, and then settling the gesture squarely on Jack.

He aimed the finger gun at Jack for a good long moment without saying anything.

"What are you doing?" Jack asked again, feeling nervous in spite of himself.

The fox mask nodded slightly in his direction.

Keeping the rifle pointed at the fox ghost, Jack turned his head slightly—then, he saw three shapes.

Jack whirled and dropped to one knee. The iron sights of the rifle lined up on the center figure, fifteen yards away in the center of the dirt road. When the figure itself fully registered, Jack's breath caught in surprise: a coyote—three coyotes, in fact.

Sores plagued all three lean, agile frames, with clumps of hair missing from the reddened edges. The wounds were caked with dried blood and covered with scratch marks. Jack knew how to identify mange in coyotes—never a comforting sight. But the familiarity of the lead coyote gave him real pause.

The creature stared at him with an empty left eye socket. Jack suspected, stomach sinking, that he'd find a familiar bullet hole in the animal's right shoulder if he looked.

Cursing the fox ghost for luring him into this trap, Jack glanced over his shoulder, unsurprised to find the masked spirit gone.

Then, all three predators exposed their yellowing teeth and growled in unison.

Jack wasn't easily scared by any stretch of the imagination, but he felt an involuntary shiver skitter down his spine. Perhaps the effects of the Memory Forest were more tangible than he initially suspected.

The lead coyote's muscles tensed.

Jack fired once at each of the ghostly coyotes, racking follow-up loads in rapid succession, then bolted down one of the side trails. He craned his head back as he ran and saw exactly what he feared—the bullets passed harmlessly through their targets.

The sound of the gun at least briefly scattered the wild dogs. But they suffered no critical damage and regrouped quickly. He knew they would be after him in moments.

If the spirits could be touched, if only by his hands, Jack knew some options for fighting remained open to him. With one coyote, he thought he could get on top of it, use his weight to hold it still, and eventually strangle the undead creature.

However, Jack could never fend off three at once. He'd get torn apart before thinning the pack at all.

Gritting his teeth, Jack slung the gun back over his shoulder and did what he hated most.

He ran.

$$\Delta$$

Jack possessed neither the speed nor the stamina of his brother, but when properly motivated, he managed a half-decent sprint.

The coyotes stayed in loose formation as they pursued him, with one occasionally breaking away and trying to hook around and cut him off. The dogs were faster, but by weaving tightly around the trees and taking sudden, sharp turns, Jack managed to keep from being entirely routed.

Ahead, one of the swampy pools of dark water gave him an idea.

Jack feinted in the opposite direction, then bolted directly toward the water. Without hesitating, he jumped into the pool—backpack, gun, and all. To his relief, the water only reached his waist.

Almost a year after Jack started working around the farm, Cash once told him about two of his hunting dogs, Shadrach and Meshach. Shadrach and Meshach were American bulldogs that each weighed about a hundred pounds. Cash raised them from puppies and trained them to hunt the wild boar that populated Nebelwood Forest. Both were strong, tough dogs—but Cash lost both of them to a single raccoon.

"How?" Jack asked. He knew raccoons were more ferocious than most people realized, but one raccoon killing two massive bulldogs who'd been trained to hunt boar stretched the limits of his belief.

"Only way he could. Strategy," Cash said, shaking his head with regret.

"What do you mean?"

"He led those dogs to a deep section of the creek and got 'em to chase him into the water."

"They couldn't swim?"

"Naw, they could swim," Buford interjected. "And they could fight. But they couldn't do both."

"That coon climbed on their heads one at a time and drowned them," said Cash, shaking his head again.

"We tried to shoot it, but we would've hit the dogs. We got him afterwards. Ol' Shadrach and Meshach didn't make it, though," said Buford.

"Got to admire the clever little cuss. Good thinking, using the terrain," Cash concluded.

Jack intended to do the same.

He raised his hands defensively and waited for the wild dogs to swim out to him. But to his surprise, they all skidded to a stop at the edge of the pool. They didn't growl or bare their teeth at him, either—they just watched Jack, in a curious and unnerving manner.

He stared back, wondering how long they would stick around if they weren't willing to enter the water.

Then the first stinging pain hit Jack's ankle and rippled through his whole leg.

An involuntary scream forced its way through Jack's clenched teeth, and he grasped at the source of the sting. Something both sticky and slippery latched onto his hand.

A moment later, his hand exploded in a wave of pain that he felt all the way to the bone.

Jack vaguely noticed more tugging sensations coming from various parts of his body, but he tried to focus on one. When he lifted his hand from the water, he screamed again.

An eel-like creature hung from the back of Jack's hand, almost two feet long and blood red, with black spots at one end of its serpentine body. There was no discernable head—but Jack felt small, hooked teeth rooting themselves in the flesh of his hand. Stubby feelers with sharp points flailed, desperately trying to get closer to his arm.

Jack watched in paralyzed horror as a small bulge moved from the back of the parasite toward the mouth burrowing in his hand. When the bulge reached the end, a small trickle of yellow liquid escaped the eel's clamped-down teeth and rolled down Jack's wrist. The rest of it went into his hand.

The second the strange bile hit his flesh, his arm pulsed with pain so overwhelming, he almost passed out.

The eldest Doe brother gritted his teeth and forced himself toward the bank of the pool, even though the coyotes were waiting for him. As he emerged from the black water, he saw that several of the parasitic creatures hung from his clothes and backpack. Fortunately, only two had found bare skin.

He raised his head and saw the three coyotes waiting just beyond the water line, teeth bared.

Jack gritted his teeth again, wrapped his hand firmly around the slick, eel-like body of the parasite, and pulled. It took a startling amount of force to pull the leech off, and blood started to flow when the hooked teeth popped free. He tossed aside the strange leech, then repeated the process for the one on his ankle.

Hurling the second parasite at the three coyotes, Jack charged out of the water in the opposite direction as they scattered. He ran farther off the main trail, pulling free the remaining leeches stuck on his clothes and bag. Whenever one popped loose, he threw it over his shoulder at the wild dogs pursuing him—like an organic grenade.

The dim light of the forest grew fainter as he ran deeper and deeper into the woods, obscuring his surroundings. Because he couldn't see, he ran squarely into an oak tree too big to wrap his arms around, nearly falling in the process. Though he managed to stay on his feet, he couldn't regain his bearings right away, and his ankle and hand both swelled from the leech bites.

Suddenly, something heavy hit him full-on at top speed, and sharp teeth scraped his shoulder. Jack hit the ground and rolled, scrambling to get on top of the coyote. Once it was beneath him, he forced his hands under the wild dog's neck to hold its snapping teeth at bay, dropping his weight to try smothering the creature.

Then, the second coyote landed on his back, biting down hard on almost the exact same spot as the first. Before Jack could react, the third coyote snapped at one of his arms, narrowly missing flesh.

Jack roared and rose to one knee, keeping the other planted on the first coyote's throat. He reached over his shoulder and grabbed the second by the neck, squeezed hard, then slammed it over his head into the dirt. Unfortunately, the throw dislodged Jack's knee from the first coyote.

The undead animal wriggled to its feet.

In desperation, Jack became a chaotic storm of fists and elbows, lashing out wildly at all three as they lunged and snapped at him. But his ankle and hand swelled to twice their normal sizes and the pain intensified, making it difficult to catch his breath.

He stumbled to his knees, and the coyotes saw their opportunity. The three ghostly canines bore down on his back simultaneously, nipping at him in a frenzy. His backpack protected him some, but the force of the attack brought him down.

As he hit the dirt, he saw something strange.

Ten yards away, a Black woman stood in a stairway, holding open what looked like an attic door. She wore a faded floral dress and a frantic expression, her dark brow wrinkled with worry.

She gestured wildly for Jack to come to her.

Jack cocked his head curiously at the strange scene, even as one of the coyotes nipped sharply at his armpit. The stairs led underground.

Jack started to crawl forward, like he was watching himself in a dream. The woman urged him on, and he stumbled to the lip of the stairs.

The coyotes followed him, occasionally darting in for a sharp nip, but once they were within her reach, the woman screamed and lashed out. The dogs yelped, scurrying back long enough for Jack to roll into the stairway.

The woman caught him before his head banged into the wooden steps. She cast one last warning glance at the coyotes, and then, she pulled the door down snugly over her and Jack.

As the door shut in the woods, all signs of the stairway disappeared. The coyotes were left staring in puzzlement at an empty patch of dirt.

They lingered a few moments, wondering if their dinner would reappear—then, they continued on their way.

Δ

Jack awoke in relative comfort. This alarmed him, so he didn't open his eyes right away. He feigned unconsciousness, trying to get a sense of his surroundings.

Clean sheets covered his body. His skin also felt fresh; his hand and ankle no longer throbbed with swollen pain. He heard the hum of a ceiling fan overhead, and somewhere in the distance, a faucet ran. Strangest of all, a powerful aroma of baked goods permeated the room.

He'd only spent a short amount of time in what William Porter called the Hinderwood, but even so, he figured bake sales weren't common.

Another sound caught Jack's attention—like something scratching against wood. As he tried to focus on it, he also picked up the faint rhythm of someone breathing nearby.

"If you don't already know where you are, I don't think you're going to figure it out by listening hard and sniffing the sheets," said a deep, pleasantly gruff voice.

Jack did not move or speak.

After a moment, the voice said, "You going to keep up the pretend sleep?"

Jack sighed and opened his eyes.

As he might have guessed, Jack found himself in a cozy bedroom. A fire burned in a small, red-brick

141

fireplace. He lay in a bed with soft, plump pillows and a hand-sewn quilt. The wooden bed frame appeared hand-carved, and a matching oak bookcase stood in one corner of the room. Next to the bookcase was a desk, and sitting at the desk was a stranger—presumably, the owner of the deep voice.

He sat uncomfortably in the desk chair, too large for its petite construction. Broad shoulders and biceps strained the fabric of his red flannel shirt. He wore jeans and weathered cowboy boots, and despite his muscular frame, Jack figured the man must be pretty old. His long, white hair matched his long, white beard.

The old man stared at Jack, and his piercing blue eyes examined him with intelligent curiosity and evident concern.

"Who are you? Where am I?" Jack asked.

The large, bearded man smiled with a warmth oddly at home on his weathered face. "My name's Ezekiel Blacklock," he said. "Welcome to the Thin House."

# INTERLUDE FOUR: MS. DUBOIS

The day after seeing Buford and Cash, Renee pulled her Buick Lesabre into the gravel circle in front of William Porter's funeral home. She took several steady breaths before opening the door, still upset that she slept so long when she only intended on a short nap. But her body needed the rest.

She hated that the boys saw her infirmity. She had been working hard to conceal her recent decline in health, particularly from those closest to her, and especially since her last doctor's visit. She knew word would get around that things had taken a turn, but she saw no sense in getting anyone worked up—especially not those who would feel it the hardest, like Buford, Cash, and the Doe boys.

The fact that Jack took one of the boys' rifles set her off, though. Not because she worried he would do something stupid with it—the boys taught him extensively about firearm safety, and Jack was easily the most responsible child she ever knew. But it broke her heart, because it meant Jack felt like he needed a gun. It meant something had happened to Jimmy.

It meant that—despite her best efforts—she had not created a safe place for her charges.

When she calmed her breathing, Renee opened her door, scooped up her handbag, and walked up the steps to the front porch. She knocked on the door and waited. After a couple beats, she knocked again. There were no sounds from inside the house.

Then, a deep voice called out, "Around the side!"

Renee walked down the front porch steps and around the side of the house.

William Porter sat in a folding chair near the door to his shed. His shovel was stuck in the ground beside him, and his big black dog lay at his feet. The dog stared stoically at Renee without barking.

Something strange about the shovel caught Renee's attention. Only half the blade was visible above ground, but there were symbols carved into its metal that she did not recognize. She wondered about the symbols and whether they might be writing from some Eastern language—but then she noticed something else by the shed door that made her heart skip a beat.

She kept her breathing level and brought her attention back to the mortician. "Good afternoon, Mr. Porter."

"It's... Renee Dubois? Sorry, I'm not very good with names, and I don't get out much."

"Yes. Ms. Dubois is fine. We've actually met before, but it was some time ago."

William Porter raised an eyebrow.

Renee smiled politely. "You made the funeral arrangements when my father passed."

"Oh yes. Louis Dubois, age 49. I remember. Well, what can I do for you today, Ms. Dubois?"

"I would like you to tell me where my sons are," she replied, her tone polite but firm.

"Your sons?"

"Jack and Jimmy Doe." She took a step closer to the mortician. "Aged fifteen and twelve. We have different last names, and they don't look much like me, but they're my sons. They've been missing since Halloween. And my next stop is the Sheriff."

"I wish I could help you, Ms. Dubois. I don't know your sons, and I haven't had any recent visitors out here."

William Porter was a practiced hand at concealing his thoughts—a necessary skill for a funeral home director. But Renee noticed his slight, uncomfortable shuffle.

She breathed softly and forced herself to remain calm.

"Then maybe you could explain to the Sheriff why that's here?" She pointed to the far edge of the shed.

William Porter followed her gesture, and she saw his eyes widen.

A small, black, leather case lay on its side a couple yards away from the door of the shack. The zipper was open, and even from where she stood, Renee could see the little slivers of metal Jimmy used to pick locks.

"I'm not sure what that is," said William Porter, flatly.

"It belongs to Jimmy. He probably used it to open that large lock sitting behind your chair. And before you lie to me again, you should know something else." She reached into her handbag and produced the photograph she'd found on Halloween night. "I've been in this town for my entire life, Mr. Porter, and I know most people here. It's a small town. But I don't know you very well. Which is strange. In fact, we haven't spoken since my father passed away. But when Jack and Jimmy said they were planning some Halloween prank here, I thought about you for the first time in years."

She held the picture out to the mortician.

William Porter took the black-and-white photograph and examined it: a pretty young woman stood beside a coffin in a church. Other people milled around in the background as well, and the mortician's gaze lingered there.

"That's me, at my father's service. And that's you, standing behind the casket." Renee paused, waiting for some acknowledgement from him. "I was *sixteen*, Mr. Porter."

Despite the age of the photo and the grainy image, William Porter could be seen quite clearly.

He looked no different from the man sitting in front of Renee—though she herself had aged nearly eighty years.

The mortician sighed.

"So, can you help me, Mr. Porter? Or should I make some phone calls?"

William Porter rose from his seat and walked around the side of the shed. Renee waited calmly until he returned, holding another folding chair.

He unfolded it, then gestured for Renee to have a seat.

"Alright then," he said. "Why not tell one more person."

Δ

Renee Dubois listened patiently as the mortician told her an impossible story. When she first discovered the photo, she suspected something out of the ordinary was afoot, but she was unprepared for the full depth of what William Porter shared.

Her heart began beating quickly when he described a hand pulling the youngest Doe brother into the shed. To keep herself calm, she rummaged through her handbag and produced one of the homemade dog treats she regularly offered the town canines. Then, she held the treat out slowly toward the big black dog, whose name she finally remembered: Ceri.

The immense animal sniffed at the baked treat but made no move to take it from her. After a moment, Ceri shifted her gaze toward Renee and licked her hand—as if to say, "No thank you, but I appreciate the gesture."

Renee shrugged and returned the treat to her bag.

To her surprise, the big dog nuzzled her gently.

When Mr. Porter finally finished his fantastic tale, he stared expectantly at Renee.

She said nothing, but the mortician sighed with irritation, so she knew her face gave away her disbelief. And before she had another chance to say anything, he rose to his feet and walked to the shed door.

Without preamble, he removed the iron bar from the handles and swung the door open.

Impossibly bright light poured from the old shed, stunning Renee. She shielded her eyes but tried to look through her fingers, squinting against the brief glimpse of brilliant light and the powerful rush of wind. Then, as quickly as William Porter opened the shed, he slammed it shut and put the barricade back into place.

He turned to Renee and waited.

Renee realized her mouth was hanging open, so she closed it quickly. Though her chest felt tight again, she cleared her throat, trying to slow her breathing.

She started to say something—and then, promptly collapsed.

$$\Delta$$

When she regained consciousness, she was lying on a couch in the funeral parlor reception area. She saw a display coffin first thing after opening her eyes, which irritated her immensely.

Though she sat up, albeit shakily, when she tried to stand, Ceri appeared and placed a gentle paw on her leg.

William Porter's voice came from across the room. "Probably best just to relax here, now."

"Where's my bag?" asked Renee.

"It's on my desk." William Porter ambled into view. "You can have it back, if you promise not to use that .38 revolver you have tucked in there."

"You sent those boys into Hell."

"No. Not quite, anyways. Just stay calm."

"Let me go in after them," she said firmly.

"Not happening. No offense, but it would only complicate things. Those boys seem capable, all we can do is give them the chance to succeed."

"Those boys are more capable than you'll ever know!" she said angrily, even if it made his point. She supposed it made some sense. Renee had trouble driving around town—she couldn't go traipsing through the afterlife.

She petted Ceri in silence until she calmed down. Then, something occurred to her. "You went through my bag."

"Yes. I apologize for invading your privacy, but I thought I might need to call somebody for you. In light of your health scare. Which is how I also came upon this." He held up the manila folder from her handbag.

Renee said nothing. She felt like what little wind she had left in her sails was quickly dissipating. Her hand, which suddenly looked very small and frail to her, rested on Ceri's head.

The big dog sighed appreciatively.

"You shouldn't have gone through those papers."

"Do the boys know the truth… about him?" the mortician asked, curiously.

"No."

"How long have they been with you?"

"Their secrets have nothing to do with you!" Renee snapped angrily.

"You're right. I'm not judging your decision. But loss like that has a way of circling around, where they are."

"I just wanted them to be kids. For just a little while."

William Porter nodded. Renee raised her head, then, and met his gaze firmly.

"But those boys are strong. They will find each other. And together, there's nothing they can't do."

"I hope you're right."

# CHAPTER NINE

Jack's gaze shifted from Ezekiel Blacklock's piercing eyes to his weathered hands—or, more specifically, to what the stranger gripped in his hands. In one, he held Jack's bat steadied across his knees. In the other, he held a large, strange-looking knife. The handle looked like some kind of bone or animal horn.

He'd apparently been using the knife to carve odd but slightly familiar symbols into the Heaven Breaker.

"What are you doing to my bat?" asked Jack.

"Based on the wounds we found on you, I'm guessing you got into some scraps lately. And weren't able to use this too well?" The big man continued his work on the bat, uncovering the white color of the ash wood beneath the black paint whenever he made a new carving.

"What are you *doing* to it?" Jack repeated, becoming irritated.

"Giving it an upgrade. Should give you better purchase, next time you swing it. How you feeling?" When he asked this last question, the old man sounded sincere, which made Jack wary.

"Good. Did you patch me up?" he asked.

"Naw, that was Eleanor." When Jack raised an eyebrow, he added, "My wife. She's getting you something to eat now."

The smell of baked goods intensified. Jack felt hungry, hungrier than he realized. The teriyaki beef MRE hadn't done much to satiate his appetite.

He stared into the man's eyes. "Who are you again?"

"My name's Ezekiel, and you're in the Thin House, our boarding house. You weren't in good shape when we found you, so Eleanor did some first aid and got you comfortable. I've just been waiting with you to make sure you didn't wake up alone."

"Boarding house?"

"Helps pay the bills. You mind if I ask you some questions, now? Because, boy, we have some big ones."

Jack shrugged then nodded.

"How did you get in our attic?"

"Was that where you found me?" Jack asked.

"Yep. I heard a thud, went upstairs, and found you passed out, with wounds you can't easily come by on this side of the veil."

The man's words made Jack sit bolt upright, and panic washed over him.

"Wait! Is this the normal world? I'm not in the Hinderwood?! I've got to get back!"

Ezekiel rose to his feet and placed a reassuring hand on Jack's shoulder.

"Easy now. We'll get everything sorted. I just need to understand what happened." He paused thoughtfully. "Did you just say you were in the Hinderwood?"

"That's what the mortician called it," Jack said, trying to calm his breathing.

Ezekiel sat on the side of the bed. He looked like he'd just been told by a credible source that the skies were raining meatballs. Then, he asked, "You know William Porter?"

"Not very well," Jack replied.

"Alright, kid. Spill it. What happened to you?"

Jack recounted the events of the past two days as best as he could. Ezekiel listened intently without interrupting. There were parts of the story—like when he mentioned spying on William Porter and the strange man in the dark suit—where he could tell Ezekiel wanted to comment, but the large, older man held his tongue until Jack finished.

"Don't that just beat all? I've never heard of a back door out of the Hinderwood, much less one leading to our attic."

"What about the woman who helped me? Is she here?" Jack asked.

"That sounds like Ms. Abigail. She's one of our permanent guests. I always thought she was confined to the attic."

"A guest? How was she in the Hinderwood? What kind of boarding house is this?"

"One with a very particular clientele," Ezekiel replied, absentmindedly, clearly thinking about something else. After a moment, the peculiar old man reached into Jack's pack, pulled out the stopwatch, and regarded the time. "It sounds like you're on a deadline, kid. We better fast track that lunch. Eleanor!"

Jack heard a smattering of footsteps as someone ascended a set of stairs, along with a second set of footsteps that, while fainter, sounded much more rapid. A moment later, a pretty woman with long, silver hair entered the room. She wore black leggings and an oversized green flannel shirt, and she held a tray stacked high with food and a tall glass of water.

She smiled brightly at Jack and started to speak, when something small and furry scampered into the room and hopped onto his bed.

In the past twenty-four hours, Jack had come face-to-face with malevolent ghosts, portals to limbo, and zombie coyotes. Despite this, he still found the sight before him to be—a little much.

Sitting at the foot of his bed was a rabbit. It regarded him with curiosity, resembling any other wild rabbit with brown-and-gray fur and oversized ears. Except for one detail.

"Does that rabbit have antlers?" Jack asked flatly.

"Chester! No! Down!" Ezekiel snapped his fingers at the creature.

The horned rabbit hopped down and sat at Ezekiel's feet.

The woman shook her head at the furry hybrid and placed the tray in Jack's lap.

"His name's Chester. He's a jackalope. Don't worry about him, he's friendly."

Jack was less concerned with the creature's friendliness and more with its sheer impossibility.

"Anyways, I didn't know what you like, so I made a little of everything: pot roast, green beans, corn-bread, some grilled chicken, roasted carrots, a fruit salad, and a slice of rhubarb pie."

"…Uh, thanks," Jack said, surprised at the impressive spread before him.

"Did we figure out how this young man ended up in the attic?"

"Apparently Ms. Abigail brought him, from the Hinderwood," Ezekiel said, then turned to Jack. "You eat up, boy."

Not waiting to be told twice, Jack dug in, eating happily while Ezekiel recounted his story to Eleanor. Jack knew that just about anything tasted great when he was starving, but the food Eleanor Blacklock gave him was truly unlike anything he'd ever eaten. Everything was delicious, with that hard-to-define home-made taste that made good food truly excellent.

And the food wasn't just filling. Jack noticed the last traces of pain and stress from his recent activities fading as he ate.

Once Ezekiel finished the story, Eleanor said, "I had no idea someone could get here from the Hinder-wood."

"Me neither. Do you think Porter knew?"

"I doubt it. Why do you think Abigail brought him here?"

"Well, you know she has a soft spot for children."

"Can I get you some more?" Eleanor asked, noticing that had Jack picked the plate clean.

Jack felt utterly stuffed and politely declined. "That might have been the best meal I've ever had," he said, earnestly.

"Oh, thank you! I'm so glad when our guests enjoy the food, and it's nice not to have any... unique dietary restrictions to keep in mind."

Jack thought it best not to ask about that last part, considering what Ezekiel mentioned about the guests.

"I really appreciate it, but I need to get going. I've been here too long as it is... I do have a question, though."

"That's understandable, you've been through a lot," said Eleanor, warmly.

"How do you two know Mr. Porter?"

The nice, strange couple shared a look. Jack didn't know much about romantic relationships, but in that moment, he could see the strong bond that Ezekiel and Eleanor shared. Without saying a word, the couple held an entire conversation in an instant.

The Doe brothers were fluent in this form of communication.

Eventually, Eleanor spoke up, giving Jack his answer. "We're in the same line of work."

"Hospitality and funeral services?" Jack raised a skeptical eyebrow.

"There's a definite overlap," Ezekiel offered. "But it may be more accurate to say that we work for the same employer."

"You mean that guy Mr. Porter was talking to?" Jack asked. He hadn't been able to see the man's face, but he remembered the sharp suit. Thinking back, the neatly-dressed man had an unmistakable air of authority, and even William Porter—who apparently wrangled evil spirits—showed deference to the strange gentleman.

"It's probably best you don't ask too many questions about him," Eleanor replied. Then, changing the subject, she said, "Now, we have a tough decision to make and not a lot of time, it seems. I imagine it wouldn't be prudent to tell you that going back into the Hinderwood is too dangerous?"

"It would not," Jack agreed.

"I understand. Family is always worth the risk. In that case, we need to figure out a way to get you back."

"If Abigail brought him here, maybe she could take him back," Ezekiel suggested.

"It's worth a try," Eleanor agreed.

Ezekiel and Eleanor left to pack up some extra food and supplies while Jack got dressed and laced up his boots. He was amazed at how good he felt, especially after the coyote and leech attacks. He felt himself wishing he could spend more time with the

Blacklocks—he knew the couple hadn't fully let on about the goings-on in their strange boarding house.

But Jack had no time to get sidetracked. Not with Jimmy still in so much danger.

Chester hadn't followed his owners out the room. The jackalope watched Jack curiously as he pulled his boots onto his feet.

Jack stared down at the rabbit hybrid for a moment, then slowly extended his hand, palm up and waiting.

Chester stared suspiciously, just for a moment, then seemed to shrug. The next thing Jack knew, the Jackalope was nuzzling his hand like a kitten.

So, Jack petted the animal gently for a moment, soaking in just a bit more of the warmth and kindness that permeated the unusual house.

Eventually, there was a knock on the door, and Ezekiel and Eleanor entered. Eleanor held Jack's backpack, and Ezekiel offered up two boxes of ammunition.

"I took the liberty of trading out some ammo for your thirty-aught-six." Ezekiel held up the boxes of bullets. "Where you're going, these should get the job done. But be careful. I probably don't need to tell you, these can hurt everyone, not just bad folks."

"Thanks," said Jack, taking the two boxes and sliding them into a side pocket of his bag.

"And I added some food and sundries to your bag," said Eleanor. "I didn't throw away those military rations, but you should consider it. Just because something's edible doesn't make it food."

Jack looked back and forth at the couple.

"I don't know if y'all are just used to people mysteriously appearing in your attic, or what, but you both seem really kind. You've made this whole thing a lot easier."

Ezekiel smiled wryly. "As someone who's been through a rodeo or two myself, it's always nice to have a helping hand. Now, let's get you to the spirit world."

Δ

Together, Eleanor, Ezekiel, Jack, and Chester left the room and trekked up the stairs. As they walked down the hallway, Jack saw several other guest rooms lining both sides of the hall, spaced evenly apart. The floors were polished hardwood, but a thick red rug ran the length of the hallway. Most doors were closed, but as they walked, Jack saw that two stood open.

When they passed the first one, Jack glanced inside out of curiosity. He saw no sign of a guest, but he noticed a wooden desk. Several books stacked on the surface all seemed to vibrate, slightly.

At the very end of the hall, next to the stairway, another door stood open. Jack didn't have to crane his head to get a curious glimpse at the occupant, because as they approached, a tall, dark figure emerged.

The man was as tall as Ezekiel but much slenderer, like a dancer. His skin was as black as coal, making his white grin all the more brilliant. The smile framed a large cigar that gave off billowing clouds of pungent smoke. He wore a black suit and tie, complete with tails, and a purple silk shirt. A matching

159

handkerchief stuck out of his front pocket. On his head, he sported an oversized top hat cocked at an angle, which made him look even taller.

Though the guest was handsome and had regal cheekbones, his features were hard to appreciate because of the paint. Jack once saw some pictures in school of Día de los Muertos celebrations, and he remembered them when he saw the man's face. The entire upper half was painted like a skull.

The hypnotic gentleman leaned against his door frame, holding a cane that ended in an ivory death's head for its handle.

"Good evening, Blacklocks! How fortuitous! I was just preparing to depart, and I hoped for a word with my generous hosts!"

"Baron," Ezekiel nodded—respectfully, Jack noticed, but not with the warmth he'd shown previously.

"We've been honored to have you join us for this year's celebration, Baron," Eleanor jumped in. "Could we meet you in the lobby in a few minutes to get you checked out?"

"I am not accustomed to showing patience. But for such wonderful hosts, I can of course make an exception." He grinned wider. "But, if I may ask, what other errand requires such haste?"

"Just have to run to the attic for a moment." Eleanor smiled, but the guest stared past her straight at Jack and blew a smoke ring.

"I don't believe we've met, young man." He extended a hand.

Jack reached for it, starting to introduce himself, but Ezekiel stepped in between him and the stranger before he could make contact.

"We'll meet you downstairs, Baron," Ezekiel said. He smiled, but there was a distinct firmness in his tone.

The guest held Ezekiel's gaze for a moment, then smiled himself. "Of course." He glanced at Jack one last time. "I'll be waiting."

The Baron bowed, turned, and walked in the opposite direction, to a set of stairs leading down— presumably, to the main floor of the boarding house.

Eleanor and Ezekiel led Jack up the stairs. Chester didn't follow. The jackalope remained in the hallway, staring after the man with the skull paint. Jack couldn't say why, but the horned rabbit reminded him in that moment of a guard dog standing watch.

"What was that about?" he asked, once they'd gotten out of earshot.

"None of our guests are bad people," said Eleanor. "But there are some whose attentions are... better off avoided."

"Especially where you're going," Ezekiel muttered.

They reached a door at the top of the stairs. Jack expected Ezekiel or Eleanor to open it, but they just stopped and shared a look.

Eventually, he cleared his throat, but the Blacklocks ignored him.

Ezekiel raised an eyebrow, and Eleanor nodded. Ezekiel sighed and turned to Jack.

"You should probably go in by yourself."

"Why?" Jack asked.

"We've only seen Ms. Abigail a handful of times… since she passed," Ezekiel explained.

"And she's never spoken to us," Eleanor added.

"She's appeared and spoken to our grandson, though. They got really close when he was little."

"You may have better luck without us," Eleanor said.

"Okay, but what do I do?" Jack asked.

"You probably won't see her at first, but she'll see you. Just tell your story," Ezekiel said. "She'll listen."

Those instructions made as much sense as anything else, and even without knowing the Blacklocks long, he trusted their judgement. So, Jack cleared his throat and adjusted his pack. "Thanks for helping me."

"Of course!" Eleanor smiled brightly, "I just wish we'd met under better circumstances."

Ezekiel clapped him on the back. "Be smart out there. The spirit world reflects the mind; remember who you are, and you'll be fine."

"I hope I can see y'all again, one day."

Eleanor hugged Jack enthusiastically. Jack was surprised to find it didn't bother him as much as hugs normally did.

"You and your brother will have to come see us once this is all sorted out."

Δ

The Blacklocks' attic was as eclectic and interesting as its owners. Jack saw several strange items scattered around the enormous room, including an ancient chest made of obsidian and pearl, a small golden statue of a goblin-like creature with eyes that followed him, and a pair of winged sandals. Besides the various artifacts and knick-knacks, he also saw seemingly endless stacks of bags and suitcases.

Only one section was free from the bizarre clutter. Sunlight streamed in through a large, arched window onto the bare floor. The whole scene felt odd—but also far from what Jack expected when the Blacklocks told him he would be confronting a ghost.

He stood by the window and stared out for a moment, unsurprised to find that the supernatural boarding house overlooked a picturesque landscape complete with a pond and a cobblestone driveway. After a moment of enjoying the view, Jack turned back to the attic.

"If you can hear me, I need your help again."

The soles of Jack's boots creaked against the wooden floorboards, and the ceiling fan whirred softly.

"I know that's why you brought me here, to help me. Get me to safety. But I wasn't alone over there."

Jack thought he felt the temperature drop slightly.

"My brother is still back there. I was trying to find him."

The room grew noticeably colder. The sun continued shining on the other side of the window, but the room itself dimmed and went dark.

"He's alive, like me, but something bad has him."

The cold licked hard at Jack's cheeks, and he saw his breath whisp out in front of him.

"If I don't go back, he'll die."

"You could die, too," said a gentle voice from over Jack's shoulder.

Jack turned. A face with kind eyes met him.

"It doesn't matter. He's my family."

Ms. Abigail stared back at him with a concern that reminded him of Ms. Dubois. "I understand," she said, and Jack wondered who she'd been before she died.

The room shifted and seemed to blur momentarily.

When Jack rubbed his eyes and looked back out the window, the scenic front yard of the Thin House was gone. Instead, he stared out the slightly-opened window at a familiar forest.

He turned back to Ms. Abigail, but she was gone.

Jack didn't hesitate. He pushed the window open and stepped back into the Hinderwood.

As the window and the Thin House vanished behind him, he heard a kind voice say, "Find your brother. And get home. While you still can."

# INTERLUDE FIVE: JIMMY

Jimmy crept around the corner of a moss-covered brick building, scanning the empty dirt road ahead of him. There were no signs of movement, just the derelict, overgrown houses and businesses surrounding the dusty street. Jimmy waited anyway. Jack taught him that patience was free, and when trying to be sneaky, it always paid well to give others the opportunity to make a mistake or reveal themselves.

After a couple minutes of dead silence and stillness, he moved quickly and smoothly to the side of the next building. Using that method, he worked his way down the street, keeping a close watch for any sign of Needlebone or the mysterious, larger monster that made the ghoul flee Main Street.

He didn't actually know where he was going. He knew he needed to get back to William Porter's shed, but he couldn't figure out where that was. He'd been in a sack for most of his journey and preoccupied with a serious wound for the remainder.

He did have one idea of how to look for the shed, though. The building with the auditorium looked… familiar. Though not his own school, it reminded Jimmy of the *old* Opossum Trot Public Elementary, which he'd seen in photos in a town history book. The school looked nearly new in that photograph—but it would have been taken in the '40s, when the town was still bustling.

The odd similarities made Jimmy wonder. Could the bizarre place around him be a dark reflection of Opossum Trot?

If so, then he knew how to get to William Porter's funeral home.

Figuring any plan to be better than no plan at all, Jimmy decided to try. As he sneaked down the equivalent of Magnolia Boulevard, he ignored the still-throbbing pain in his hand and focused on moving quietly, the way Jack showed him.

A few minutes later, he heard a second set of footsteps.

When he stopped walking, another pair of small feet abruptly came to a rest behind him. He remembered the short, dark shadows of the creatures in the window—Needlebone called them "The Empty Ones"—and without hesitation, Jimmy ran.

A small voice on the edge of tears called out, "Wait! Please!"

Jimmy instinctively skidded to a halt and glanced back.

Yards away, a little girl with blond, nearly-white hair peeked out from behind a crumbling café with a tree growing out its window. She wore a frilly but faded nightgown, and though Jimmy suspected her slippers once smiled up at her as kindly sheep or rabbits, the muddy clumps of fuzz would never be recognizable again. And even from a distance, Jimmy saw long streaks of wet tears streaming down her cheeks.

Before he could say anything, she begged, "Please help me, I'm scared," in a soft voice that echoed through his soul.

Though he'd already seen plenty strangeness and violence in the bizarre shadow world, Jimmy could not turn away from someone who needed help. Neither Jack nor Ms. Dubois had raised him to ignore that kind of plea.

He turned back and walked toward the little girl. "It's okay. Don't be afraid."

"I'm lost!" She burst into fresh tears. "I was walking across the street with my mom, then everything turned black, and now I can't find her anywhere. I want to go home!"

Suddenly, Jimmy remembered—Needlebone had called this place "Heaven."

So, Jimmy said, "I'm sorry." It was all he could say.

"I want to go home," she repeated.

"Me too," he agreed. Then, curiously, "How long have you been here?"

"Thirty-seven days. I counted. I can count past a hundred." She offered the last detail with sudden pride.

"Where are you from?"

"Shreveport." Her reply sounded meaningless to her, like a parent just made her repeat the answer until it sealed in her memory.

"Louisiana, huh? I guess this place is bigger than just Opossum Trot."

"What are you talking about?" The little girl raised an eyebrow.

"I'm from a place called Opossum Trot, Mississippi. I didn't realize that all of this—" He gestured at the dark world around them. "—was bigger than my town."

"Do you know a way home?"

"Maybe. I was pulled in here through an old shed. When the doors opened, a lot of light came out and a monster pulled me in."

Almost absently, the girl said, "Oh, I know where that is."

"What? You know where the shed is?" Jimmy asked with sudden interest.

"It's not a shed," she replied, matter-of-factly. "But I know about a place in the woods where a door is, sometimes, and I've heard others say white light comes out."

"Do you know how to get there?"

"Yeah, it's not very far." She tugged at a strand of thread sticking out from her gown.

"You have to take me there! I think it can get us home."

At that, the girl perked up. "Really! You promise?" Her face exploded with excitement.

"I think so. That's how I got here, anyways. It stands to reason, we should be able to get out," Jimmy offered.

"I'll take you there if you'll let me go home with you. I could find my mama!"

"It's a deal," Jimmy agreed.

Without another word, she led him west into the woods.

$$\Delta$$

Needlebone referred to the woods as some kind of afterlife, but Jimmy wasn't so sure. Despite seeing so many monsters and unexplainable phenomena, he hardly trusted Needlebone to have told him the truth.

And yet… a nagging feeling insisted that Needlebone told him a near-truth.

It made him wonder about the little girl. Was she someone who ended up in the wrong place, like him? Or was she some kind of spirit? And if so… what would that mean when they tried to leave?

Jimmy pushed those thoughts from his mind. After all, he needed to find a way out, first and foremost. He decided to pass the time with small talk.

"What's your name?"

"Cecilia," she said, without looking up at Jimmy. She seemed to be scanning the area.

"How long have you been here?" Jimmy asked.

She ignored the question and pointed up ahead. "Look, there's the way."

A couple yards ahead, a particularly large oak tree stood rooted right off the cobblestone road—easily the largest tree he'd ever seen, even in Opossum Trot.

But the tree's size hardly struck Jimmy, compared to its face.

The face was not carved into the wood but raised out of it, as if someone placed a mold on the tree when it was young, and the bark grew into the shape of the face over time. The visage made Jimmy think of the Easter Island statues. Small slits of eyes stared out from under an expansive brow, and its thin lips pursed tightly. An equally thin nose protruded from the trunk of the tree. Folds of wrinkles gave the face an ancient, wizened quality.

"What is that?" Jimmy asked.

"One of the King's Roads," said Cecilia, walking toward the strange tree.

"King's Roads?"

Cecilia sighed, sounding a little impatient. "This place has lots of kingdoms. Roads were made for those who govern them, but many have been forgotten."

Her answer didn't clarify anything for Jimmy. He wanted to ask her to elaborate, but she furtively scanned the area once again. "What's wrong?"

"I know how to use it, but it's a secret." Still holding his hand, Cecilia led him toward the tree, positioning them right in the face's line of sight.

The tree didn't look very healthy to Jimmy. A dark, orange fungus grew on the large, intricate root system, and when he stood close to the trunk, he saw a network of insect tunnels weaving through the damp bark. Jimmy watched as some kind of bug—a cross between a cockroach and a centipede—skittered from one small opening to another. At first glance, the creature looked too bulky to fit into the tunnel, but its soft, bulging frame managed to force its way smoothly through.

"How do you use it?" Jimmy asked, trying not to gag.

Cecilia said nothing, reaching up to one of the lower hanging limbs and pulling off a small branch. The stick wasn't particularly large, and it broke away with the smooth "crack" of long-dead wood. One end came to a sharp, natural point.

Jimmy asked, "What are you...?"

Before he finished, Cecilia jabbed the sharp end of the stick into her own index finger.

"Hey!" Jimmy yelled in surprise. "Why did you do that?"

"The King's Roads are old. They're weak and hungry. If you want to use them, you have to feed them."

Before Jimmy could ask any more questions, Cecilia squeezed her bleeding finger and rubbed it on the tree, smearing a dark stain across the thin lips of the oak's face. Jimmy thought the smear looked unusually dark compared to the blood stains he'd seen throughout his life. When he looked at Cecilia's hand, he saw that her blood wasn't red at all, but a dark blue ooze.

Then, the massive tree began to move.

The slits Jimmy previously took for eyes expanded until two jagged hollows stared down at the youngest Doe brother. The holes briefly made him think of *To Kill a Mockingbird,* when Boo Radley left presents for Scout and Jem in the knothole. However, Jimmy figured if he put a hand into either of the hollowed-out gaps in front of him, he'd likely lose several fingers.

As he watched, the tightly pursed lips also parted, revealing a colossal maw of sharp branches like canine teeth. The grin leered at Jimmy like a jack-o-lantern so large, Jimmy could have walked through it—straight into the interior of the oak tree.

This seemed exactly Cecilia's intent.

The small girl in the nightgown lifted one foot still covered in a dirty slipper, and she stepped into the tree. She reached back for Jimmy's hand.

"Where does it go?" he asked.

"It'll take us to the door. To go home," she said.

Jimmy was not interested in stepping into the mouth of a blood-eating tree. He didn't understand what Cecilia meant when she talked about the King's Roads. Ever since Needlebone grabbed him, Jimmy felt like he'd been thrown from one unfathomable situation to another with no good decisions to make.

But he felt like he was finally in a place where he could at least make some basic decisions—like whether or not to follow a strange little girl through a malicious-looking tree mouth.

"I'm afraid to go alone," said Cecilia, her voice small.

Jimmy sighed. "You've used this before?"

"Yes."

"Okay."

Jimmy took her hand and stepped inside, treading carefully around the sharp, teeth-like branches.

Cecilia led him down a long path, far too long to be inside an oak tree, no matter how large. The longer they walked, the more darkness descended. When he turned around to look behind him, Jimmy saw the jagged mouth of the tree close.

Since Cecilia kept walking without worry, he tried not to think about it.

To his surprise, a pale, green light appeared. Looking up, Jimmy found a multitude of worms crawling on the interior walls of the pass. A faint light emanated from their wriggling bodies.

They walked almost a full minute before coming to a wall.

A tapestry of interconnected symbols had been carved deep into the wood: a drawing of a woman with half her body painted black; another drawing of a skull wearing a top hat and smoking a cigar. One strange image showed a fiery lion with flies buzzing about its imposing frame. And there were many others, all sharing one detail in common—every drawing was encircled and linked by thick, spiraling lines.

Cecilia pointed to the symbol of a gnarled tree surrounded by an expanse of swirling lines. "We're here."

"Where's Mr. Porter's shed?" Jimmy asked.

Cecilia stood on her tiptoes and reached out with her still-bloody finger toward the top of the tapestry. Before Jimmy could get a clear look, she pressed against one of the topmost symbols. The collage of carvings suddenly disappeared, replaced by a new, dark opening.

Cecilia didn't hesitate. She led Jimmy into the darkness.

Jimmy expected another long passage of damp dirt and bark walls. Instead, his first step touched down on solid stone, and as his eyes adjusted to the pale, faint light, he saw a rocky plain. Dozens of curved stones scattered through choking weeds, the only plant life in view. Jimmy stood on a flat rock, one of several that created a path leading to a tall, thin structure in the distance. The entire plain dropped sharply off at the horizon, as if carved into the side of cliff.

"This doesn't look like what I remember," Jimmy said.

"It doesn't?" Cecilia stared at him with an exaggerated expression of shock, something harsh and mocking in her tone.

Jimmy raised an eyebrow. "No…"

Glancing behind her, he saw another tree like the one they'd entered. The mouth was closed, and its expression was solemn. He shifted his gaze back to Cecilia.

Since they first met, her expression had remained timid and mild—but standing on the flat rock, she grinned at Jimmy, almost viciously.

The grin was neither warm nor good-humored, but savoring, like the grin of someone reveling in a practical joke taken too far. And as Jimmy stared at her, he thought he saw far too many teeth in her smile.

"Cecilia?" he said, slowly backing away from the little girl he'd been trying to rescue.

"Wait, Jimmy, hold my hand!"

Cecilia reached for Jimmy's hand.

As she did, her arm and fingers stretched until they were disproportionately long. Her nails turned yellow, sharp, and jagged.

Jimmy gasped and stumbled backward. When he lost his balance and almost fell, the monstrous hand caught him firmly by the wrist. The grip was so strong, it felt like the bones in his forearm would splinter, and the dirty, yellow fingernails cut into his skin.

He tried to pull free, forcing himself to look up.

Only faint aspects of Cecilia remained, all quickly disappearing. The floral print dress faded into threadbare, pattern-less trousers covering impossibly skinny legs. The sandy blond hair receded into a pale, scarred head, until only a few wispy strands remained. Where slippers once covered small, dainty toes, disintegrating

175

strands of fabric did nothing to hide the long, thin, and scabbed feet that hadn't known shoes for a long, long time.

The familiar voice cackled maniacally, *"Please help me!"*

"No!" Jimmy screamed, but it was too late.

The Needlebone Man hit him sharply on the side of the head—and then, darkness.

# CHAPTER TEN

Jack spent two hours searching for the road where the coyotes attacked him, and by his count, he also lost about six hours resting at the Blacklocks'. According to Porter's stopwatch, less than twenty-four hours remained for him to find Jimmy and return home.

Growing up, Jack was never fast like Jimmy. Running hadn't been an option for him, so he learned to fight. But with no idea how much farther he'd need to go to reach the Edge and find Needlebone, with no solid idea of the time it would take to get there and back, with little certainty that he even knew the best direction to go, Jack realized he'd need every advantage in order to make it, to find Jimmy in time.

He began to run.

When he was too tired to run, he jogged. When the muscles in his legs burned from the inside out, he walked. While he walked, he drank some water and ate one of the peanut-butter-and-honey sandwiches Eleanor packed for him. Then, he ran again.

As he traveled, the occasional brilliant beams of light from the east reassured him. He also noticed gradual changes to his surroundings. As the dark, fog-riddled world blurred past, the forest took on a barren quality. The immense spiderlike oaks became rarer and rarer, replaced infrequently with trees all devoid of leaves and scorched from some previous fire. The green moss that previously carpeted the forest floor disappeared, swapped out for swampy, black mud.

Though the fog remained, the flat, deforested landscape allowed Jack to see farther into the distance. After three hours of running, Jack noticed two odd things on the horizon.

First, a smooth, white wall made of ivory or pearl stretched across the barren landscape as far as the eye could see. The wall's sharp contrast with the blackened landscape of its surroundings created a bizarre, off-putting image. Jack's dirt road led to a small gap in the white wall, the only one visible for miles.

And then, though the strange barrier startled him, Jack grew more concerned with a second peculiar sight.

A figure stood in the road, just before the gap in the wall.

Jack unslung the rifle from his shoulder and raised the scope to his eye. His finger instinctively rested on the trigger guard, but he made no move to switch off the safety button. The scope brought the figure a little closer, close enough for Jack to see a shock of orange and olive green, but not much else. So, he adjusted the optic's magnification and brought the figure into sharper focus.

The picture cleared up just in time for Jack to see the fox ghost wave at him—with a sardonic twitch of his wrist.

Jack considered pulling the trigger, but he remembered Buford's warning and hesitated.

The fox ghost had been following him all along. He'd been there when Jimmy was taken, when Jack first entered the Hinderwood, and when the coyotes attacked. Jack wanted answers—and shooting the stranger in the fox mask wouldn't get him any.

Jack lowered the gun, but he didn't sling it back over his shoulder. He held the rifle in front of him and walked toward both the figure and the white wall.

He came to a stop about a hundred yards from the boy in the fox mask. He aimed the gun and put his finger on the safety button. The fox ghost did not seem concerned. He took a deep breath and stretched, as if yawning behind the painted mask.

"I got some new bullets that I'm pretty sure can ruin your day, so don't get any ideas," Jack warned. "Now, why are you following me?"

The fox ghost turned his head to the left, then to the right, as if looking both ways. Then, he looked back at Jack and raised his hands—as if to say, "I've actually been here a while."

Jack's shoulders squared and tensed. "You know what I mean! You've been around for this whole stupid thing! Now talk!" he shouted. "Who are you?"

The spirit raised a hand and pointed at the fox mask. Jack waited for more, but the ghost just stared expectantly.

"What does that mean?"

The fox ghost sighed and shook his head slightly.

Then, Jack watched in surprise as the spirit shrugged, turned around, and started to walk away.

"Hey!" Jack shouted in protest. "Get back here!"

The masked boy continued to walk toward the gap in the wall at a comfortable, deliberate pace.

"Stop!" Jack yelled.

The ghost in the fox mask didn't turn around, but he made a rude gesture for Jack's benefit.

"Jerk," Jack muttered, running toward the spirit.

In the wall's gap, Jack saw a deep shadow, a thick darkness—like someone dyed the ever-present fog an inky black. The fox ghost stopped just before the shadow and cast one last look at Jack.

Then, with Jack still several yards away, the painted eyes of the mask slipped into the black.

Jack skidded to a stop in front of the shadowy opening. He couldn't see anything past the threshold. Removing a flashlight from his backpack, he shined the beam into the crevasse—but the light could not penetrate the thick darkness.

Jack glanced at the face of the stopwatch, groaned in frustration, then stepped into the gap.

For just a moment, Jack felt an all-encompassing physical panic, the kind of instant shock that comes from suddenly missing a step and falling. He still stood upright, but in darkness so complete, his equilibrium faltered. Jack tried to step backward into the light outside the gap, but there was no sign of the trail, the wall, or anything—nothing, except for the consuming abyss.

He fumbled in the darkness, struggling to focus his thoughts, to keep track of the time as it passed. Eventually, he was vaguely aware of getting on his hands and knees, blindly feeling for the edge of a wall or for anything that would give him a sense of his location. Despite his best efforts, he found no landmarks that gave shape to the infinite, supernatural shadow.

Jack growled angrily and began lashing out in every direction.

"There's only one way out."

In the pitch black, Jack wasn't entirely sure whether the voice was real or imagined.

"Whether you want to go back the way you came or continue to a certain, torturous death, there is only one way out."

Jack slowed his breathing and tried to find the source of the voice, with no luck.

"Are you ready?" the voice asked.

Jack sighed. "Sure."

A loud clicking sound made Jack flinch. Suddenly, a spotlight appeared ahead of him. The weight of the darkness seemed to lessen, and he knew he would be able to walk forward into the ring of light. He paused, though, confused by what he saw there.

Inside the spotlight, a folding table waited with a portable chess board on top. Though the board itself looked cheap and flimsy, the playing pieces were high-end: the black set, a polished marble, the white ones all carved ivory. An empty chair sat between Jack and the black set's side of the board. Across the table on the white side, a man sat waiting.

"Care for a game?" he asked.

He wore jeans and a black, hooded sweatshirt with the sleeves pushed up to reveal ropy, muscular forearms. A baseball cap sat on his shaved head, and a pair of dirty, military-issue boots covered his feet. He sat straight, with good posture but a relaxed demeanor, his observant eyes piercing through Jack.

He smiled without any warmth or humor, then motioned for Jack to be seated.

"No."

"Pardon me?" The man raised an eyebrow.

"I don't have time for games," Jack replied.

"We all got time here, kid. What's your rush?"

"I've got to find my brother and get back before we get stuck here," said Jack, evenly.

"Stuck here?" The man reached into the pocket of his sweatshirt and produced a pair of glasses. Once he put them on his face, he stared at Jack.

"Well, I'll be... you're alive." The man seemed legitimately concerned. "What are you doing here, kid? This place is dangerous." Then, his eyes rested on the rifle slung over Jack's shoulder. "Maybe you already know that."

Jack ignored his concern and his comments. "How do I get out of here?" he asked, gesturing at darkness surrounding them.

"If you want, I can turn you around the way you came," he said, before nodding at the game in front of him. "But you got to beat me if you want to keep going. And if you lose, you'll be trapped in that darkness you crawled out of for as long as... well, I don't know exactly. But I've never seen anyone come out."

"Just let me through," Jack demanded.

"Not up to me. The only way the door opens is for you to play. But look, kid, you really don't want to keep going that way. All that's on the other side of this wall is a deranged monster and the abyss."

"Please."

"No. Besides, you still ain't answered my question. What's a living boy like you doing in this place?"

Jack had neither time nor patience for explanations. "There's no way past, unless I play?"

"Yes, but—"

Before the man could ask any more questions, Jack stepped forward and sat in the empty seat.

"Dang it, kid," the man sighed, taking off the glasses and rubbing his eyes. When he slid the glasses back on, Jack thought he looked oddly familiar. The man stared back at Jack for a moment, shook his head, then gestured for Jack to make his first move. "Don't say I didn't warn you," he muttered.

Jack learned to play chess from a pair of old men who met up in City Park once a week. He considered himself a fair opponent, in the same way he considered himself a fair shot with a rifle. He'd witnessed greatness in both, and he knew his limitations. Though he'd never been able to teach Jimmy, Ms. Dubois was fairly adept, and they played some evenings after dinner—when she was feeling up to it.

Jack most enjoyed playing with Scott. Scott was an avid study of chess strategy and always introduced him to new, complex theories. Jack never won against him, but he always had fun with the game.

When he sat across from the man in the sweat-shirt, however, he was not interested in a fun match. He needed it to end quickly, so he could pass through the wall and find Jimmy.

He decided to try the Scholar's Mate. When employed successfully, the Scholar's Mate produced a checkmate in four moves. Jack learned the sequence from one of the two old men in City Park, a retired professor.

The professor remarked on Jack's quiet, stoic personality and said, "You've got the right temperament for this game. But, if you're ever in a hurry and playing a nitwit, try this."

Jack moved the pawn in front of his queen, to space E4, in the middle of the board.

The man in the hoodie moved a black pawn to meet him.

Without missing a beat, Jack moved the bishop to the right of his king, to space C4. The bishop stood in the middle of no man's land, one space over from his pawn.

"Ain't gonna be that easy, kid."

Jack felt like groaning, but he didn't want to give anything away. The Scholar's Mate was still a good set up for his favored strategy, even if it didn't work on its own. He typically used his queen to pick off his opponents' pieces until he forced them into a corner, but that strategy took more time, and he'd hoped to get out of the game quickly.

"Did I hear you say you were looking for your brother?"

"Let's just play the game," Jack replied.

He cut across the center with his queen and took a black pawn. To his surprise, the man in the hoodie moved a rook across the board, attacking his queen with a knight for reinforcements. If Jack attacked the rook, the knight would take his queen.

To make matters worse, his own king stood directly behind the queen. Jack felt something drop in the pit of his stomach. If he moved the queen to safety, he would put himself in check.

He looked up into the face of his opponent, and the man smiled.

"You can't win that way. Trying to defeat an army by yourself is an exercise in futility. Got to use all your resources."

Jack was too frustrated to reply. He shook his head in resignation and moved to take the rook.

When the black knight took his queen, he gritted his teeth angrily, beyond upset with himself. Losing the queen so early was a rookie mistake for anyone—but for someone with an aggressive style like his, it was almost catastrophic.

"Calm down, kid. The game's bigger than one piece."

"Shut up!" Jack roared, surprised by the sudden rush of fury. But the shock did nothing to stunt the hot flash of anger that coursed through his wiry frame. He felt everything that happened to him and Jimmy over the past two days hitting him all at once, and he'd had enough. "I told you I don't care about this stupid game! You're wasting my time!"

Jack reached for his bat, then, ready to fight his way past the infuriating gatekeeper, but he did not feel the familiar ash handle in its sheath. In fact, for the first time, he realized the entire pack was gone. The ring of light surrounded only him, the man, and the game of chess.

But Jack didn't let that stop him. He flipped the table over and lunged toward his opponent. The board and the pieces flew into the air for just a moment—then fell perfectly back into place. Jack himself landed back in his seat, everything wholly reset.

Jack glared up at the man, who just shrugged. "I told you, kid, there's only one way. Once you sit down, we're locked in."

The eldest Doe brother tried to calm down. There was nothing to gain in wasting time. So, he looked at his pieces and tried to come up with a new strategy.

Both his knights remained on the board, reminding him of the last game he played with Scott. He remembered how Scott used them, how the two pieces worked in harmony, simultaneously attacking his pieces while defending each other's positions. The strategy had been formidable; perhaps it would help him.

Jack brought his knights into play. He progressed cautiously, making sure to use them as a team rather than as individual pieces. Using Scott's strategy, he managed to slow his opponent's advances and, eventually, forced him on the defensive.

When Jack captured his opponent's bishop, the man chuckled. "That's more like it. Two knights can do a lot of damage. They've always been my favorite pieces." He said so thoughtfully, almost to himself.

Both his chuckling and his reminiscent demeanor increased Jack's sense that he knew the man, somehow. He couldn't quite place it, but his features—particularly in the eyes and the brow—reminded him of someone.

But it didn't matter. Jack shook his head and returned his attention to the board.

Scanning the field, he tried to formulate a path to checkmate. With his recent advance, Jack created an opening to the king on the second-to-last row, near the corner. Only a white knight hovered nearby as a guard, with a rook waiting on the back row.

Jack moved one of his knights to cut the king off from advancing.

His opponent brought his last rook out of the corner, standing it behind the king.

Jack stared at the board—eyes purposefully scrunched, as if trying to find a move in vain. Eventually, he shrugged and moved his rook forward on the opposite side of the board, claiming a pawn.

"Taking potshots?" the man asked. He moved his king backward diagonally, to the left of his rook, so the castle faced one of Jack's knights in a head-on attack.

"No," Jack replied. He moved his own rook down the field and put the king in check.

To his surprise, the man smiled.

"That's good," he said. "Two pieces working in harmony can accomplish a lot. Three can win you a battle."

He observed the board for a moment, then moved his knight next to his king, blocking the rook's attack. If Jack took the knight with his rook, the king would counter-attack.

Instead, Jack grinned, taking the white knight with his spare black knight.

Again, the man smiled.

Jack thought he seemed awfully cavalier, for someone about to lose. He stared at the man, the recently claimed white knight in his palm, feeling something strange, as if he were missing something.

Then, he started suddenly.

He'd taken several pieces over the course of the game, all with a solid heft and the cool feel of smooth ivory. The knight he held felt different.

When he opened his hand and stared down at the knight, Jack realized the piece was made of solid white plastic—not ivory.

He quickly surveyed the other pieces on the board and confirmed that all the others showed the organic grain of real ivory. His black pieces all bore a uniform appearance of black marble. As he viewed the remaining ivory knight with renewed curiosity, Jack realized it looked familiar—as familiar as the man himself.

Jack's breath caught, and all the clues fell into place.

He looked at the man again. "This knight isn't part of the set," he said, slightly raising the plastic knight in his hand. "You're missing a piece."

"It's not missing. It's on loan," the man replied. He focused on the game board, busy formulating a new strategy.

"To your son. Right, Mr. Eldridge?"

"What did you say?" The man's tone grew suddenly serious, a mixture of shock and wariness.

"Scott. He's the one who taught me to use the knights like this."

Drew Eldridge stared at Jack in increasing surprise.

"We're friends," Jack explained. Then, he reached into a pocket of his coat. "He let me borrow this for good luck."

Jack set a white knight made of ivory onto the table. There was a small chip in its ear.

Both players sat silently for a long time. Then, the tired-looking man reached out and picked up the chess piece. He cradled it in his hands like a baby bird and sighed deeply. A weight seemed to lift from him.

"You're waiting for him, aren't you? Before passing on?" Jack asked.

"I was only there for such a small part of his life," said Drew Eldridge, sadly. "The least I can do is make sure he doesn't start the next part by himself."

Jack understood. "Seems like he'd have a hard time finding you out here."

"I don't spend much time here," he explained. "Just have to show up when people pass through the gap. There's got to be a challenger—otherwise, people just wander in the dark. With me here, I can at least get most of them to turn back."

"I can't turn back. I won't leave my brother here."

"Your brother never came by me. Which means he was taken the back way by Needlebone. You know who that is?"

Jack nodded.

"Then you know there's nothing but death past these walls. Not just death of the body, either. Death of everything that makes you who you are. That's where you want to go?"

"That's what I want to save my brother from," said Jack, softly.

"Then let's finish the game." The man advanced a pawn on the opposite side of the board.

Jack knew right away, it was a meaningless move—yet, it couldn't have had more meaning.

He moved one of his knights and said, "Check."

"And mate," Scott's dad finished. "Well played."

The spotlight that encircled the table expanded, illuminating a narrow path bisecting the table. One direction led back the way Jack came. The second led through the other side of the wall.

Jack could only see a narrow view of the landscape on the other side, but the terrain became mountainous and rocky. He also noticed that, even though the entirety of the Hinderwood had been dimly lit, the farther side of the wall made the former seem brighter by comparison.

"The path continues for about a mile before you hit Needlebone's territory. You'll know it when you see it. Be careful, though, Needlebone's lair ain't all that's out there. His place butts up against the Edge. If you go over the side, you'll be lost forever. In a place even worse than this."

"Yes, sir. Thanks," Jack replied.

"Can I give you some advice, kid? About what comes next?"

"Yes, sir."

"I get the feeling you live like you play. You put a lot on yourself and rely on your own capabilities, which may be substantial, since you're the first living kid I've seen make it all the way out here. But trust me, it won't be enough. This place—" He gestured all around them. "—can only be survived if you're willing to change."

Jack said nothing. The man continued.

"Use all your resources, just like you did at the end of the game, and you and your brother might make it out of this place."

Jack nodded. "Can I offer you some advice?"

"Lay it on me."

"You're not the first good person I've met here. But only the monsters seem to stick together. If you and people like you are waiting here, why wait alone?"

The man seemed to consider this. Eventually, he nodded. "Worth thinking about."

Jack rose from his seat and thought of something else. "Hey, did you say that no one else tried to come this way recently?" he asked.

"Yeah, but the Needlebone Man has a secret way for taking his prisoners."

"I wasn't wondering about him," Jack replied, shaking his head. "I was wondering about a guy in a fox mask. I saw him on the trail right before I came in."

"Fox mask? No, I haven't heard of anyone like that. And no one came in before you. But we spirits can have an easier time traveling through this world. We aren't bound to the limitations of our perceptions. Just because it seemed like he came through the path ahead of you, doesn't mean he actually did."

Jack nodded. He started to walk toward the darker of the two paths, but Scott's father placed a hand on his shoulder.

"Wait." He reached down to the pieces. For a moment, Jack thought he was going to return the white knight. Instead, he picked up one of the black knights and held it out. "My son will recognize it. Tell him I've got another game in me, but there's no rush. I'll be waiting."

# INTERLUDE SIX: THE NEEDLEBONE MAN

When the Needlebone Man reached the tower that served as his home, the boy remained unconscious in his grip. Though the youngest Doe brother's sleeping form weighed nothing at all to the thin, pale monster, it would sustain him for a long time—longer than any prey in recent memory. After shifting the boy's weight, he pushed the heavy, wooden door to the ancient tower open, greeted by the familiar sight of a tall and narrow stairway.

The monster was not deterred. He whistled merrily as he ascended the steep steps.

"Needlebone" was not truly his name. His real name had been forgotten. But the other spirits began referring to him as "the Needlebone Man" long ago, when he first grew carnivorous. The gardens outside his tower were relatively small, then, but he'd built a fearsome reputation, nonetheless. He decided to encourage the moniker.

The decision proved wise. His infamy spread from the Edge all the way to the bordering kingdoms that were virtually unknown to most spirits in the Hinderwood. In a world of monsters, he'd become the most famous, the most feared. Or at least, close to the most feared. The Pursuer threatened all the residents of the Hinderwood, including Needlebone, but the Entity never traveled far enough west to endanger the monster's personal sanctuary. No, the barren lands at the Edge belonged to him and him alone. There, the pale monster enjoyed a wide berth to feed and cultivate his garden.

When he finally reached the first room at the top of the staircase, he heard the boy's breathing change slightly. He would be waking soon—and this pleased Needlebone.

Stopping in the threshold of the first room, Needlebone looked up at the remaining stairs. The tower only contained two rooms: one above, where he slept on the rare occasions that he needed rest, and the one in front of him, which served as his workroom and pantry. A massive table filled most of the space. Next to it, a workbench displayed a collection of surgical instruments, all in varying stages of rust. A tall shelving unit leaned against the opposite wall.

After entering the workroom, Needlebone dropped Jimmy roughly onto the table.

Then, his eyes instinctively shot to the shelves, which held approximately twenty-two glass jars with rubber-stopped lids. Each jar contained different amounts of a fine, red dust that made Needlebone twitch with something close to hunger. He counted the jars twice to make sure none had gone missing since the last count.

Then, he returned his attention to the youngest Doe brother.

Thick ropes wound through pre-drilled holes in the table, and Needlebone used these to secure the boy. Because one of the boy's hands had swollen so large, Needlebone worried briefly that he would need more rope. But he found he was able to manage, even if he couldn't tighten the knot to his usual standards.

Then, Needlebone patted the boy down and checked his pockets. He found a couple pieces of food and, to his surprise, a portion of a preserved rabbit's foot attached to a small chain. Looking closely, he saw some blood from the boy's wound had stained its fur. He wondered briefly at the strange nick-knack, then tossed it onto his work bench.

That task completed, he set to assembling the Apparatus.

Needlebone was not an inventor, nor was he naturally skilled at using tools. He'd assembled various surgical instruments over years and years of scavenging the Hinderwood and, through trial and error, he'd discovered their value in breaking down his victims. But he couldn't take credit for the Apparatus's creation. That honor belonged to the Gentleman.

Needlebone had been in the Hinderwood for a lifetime, perhaps many lifetimes—he couldn't really remember. He'd been there when the King's Roads saw regular traffic. He'd been there so long, that he'd forgotten the limitations of his own body. Though, that particular side effect of his age came with benefits. Hunting proved easier when he could make himself look like prey. He'd been there long enough to see and to learn. The Hinderwood held few secrets for the Needlebone Man.

But even so, the Gentleman remained a mystery.

He'd appeared shortly after Needlebone discovered the barren lands. At the time, Needlebone was scrounging his then-small garden for something to eat. He settled on an ankle bone with faint traces of essence still lingering in the marrow. As he gnawed, a polished voice behind him made him flinch.

"There's a better way."

Needlebone whirled around, dropping the bone and baring his teeth.

A well-dressed man wearing white gloves sat comfortably on a nearby rock. He smiled politely at Needlebone.

"Who are you?"

The man ignored the question. "You won't last very long doing it that way," he said. He pointed at the bone riddled with chew marks.

Needlebone stood up straight and took a step toward the Gentleman. "Foolish to come to Needlebone's home," he said. "Now, it will become your home."

He reached for the Gentleman, but in that moment, the man no longer sat on the rock. Instead, he stood a couple yards away, leaning nonchalantly against a withered tree. He seemed amused by Needlebone's threat.

"The problem is that you are approaching the work like an animal," he said. "When a tiger kills, it feeds with no thought beyond the current meal. When its belly is full, it leaves to rest. The tiger may return to the carcass much later when it hungers again, but by then, much of the kill is spoiled, or perhaps has been claimed by another. Either way, there is little nourishment to be gained during a second feeding, and nothing at all by the third. Do you understand?"

Needlebone did not understand, but he was intrigued.

"A butcher, on the other hand, thinks long term," continued the Gentleman. "He uses his skill and his tools to pick the bones clean, to harvest all the meat in preparation for future hunger. Predators eventually die hungry; butchers live long and grow fat."

"I don't want to be fat," replied Needlebone, thinking the excess weight would make him slow and vulnerable.

"I'm not telling you how *much* to eat, only that you don't have to go hungry," said the Gentleman, with a trace of impatience.

"How?" asked Needlebone, curious in spite of himself.

"With this." The Gentleman nudged a large box sitting on the ground near his foot.

Needlebone wondered why he hadn't noticed it before. "What is it?"

"A machine. A side venture, if you will. I have an abundance of time on my hands, after all. I'm sure you understand." When Needlebone said nothing, he continued. "It will allow you to… preserve and savor your prey. And I am of a mind to give it to you and show you how to use it."

"Why would you help Needlebone?" asked the tall, thin monster, distrustfully.

"Oh, but you would be helping *me*. Am I right in surmising that you have made this place your home?" He gestured at the barren lands around them.

Needlebone grinned. "My kingdom."

"Indeed. Well, if you are willing to guard and maintain this 'kingdom,' I will give you the machine. I will also make it so that as long as you rule this land, only those of your… particular taste may enter."

"What?"

"Children, Mr. Needlebone. As long as you are king of this land, only you and the children may enter. Do you accept these terms?" He leaned forward, then, and even though Needlebone was significantly taller, the gentleman in the gray suit seemed to tower over him.

For a moment, Needlebone felt uncomfortable—almost nervous—but then, he thought about everything being offered and what it would mean for him.

"Why do you want this?" he asked, suspiciously.

"There is power in controlling borders, even here," he said, producing a handkerchief and wiping his mouth. Needlebone noticed a damp, red spot growing on the white cloth.

He looked out toward the empty abyss. "But there's nothing else out here."

"For now, I'd like to keep it that way," he said. "Now, Mr. Needlebone, do we have a deal?"

Needlebone did not need much time to debate. "Yes," he rasped.

The Gentleman smiled, then, revealing a mouth full of blood-stained teeth. "Excellent."

Even after the Gentleman showed Needlebone how to use the machine, it took him years to become a skilled operator—but everything was as the Gentleman assured him it would be. Furthermore, the Gentleman made good on his other promises. Shortly thereafter, a wall of polished bone appeared across the barren lands, and no spirits besides those of his victims seemed capable of passing through it.

The Gentleman's gifts allowed him the security and safety to flourish. No more did he prey meal-to-meal, no, he used the Gentleman's Apparatus to stockpile pure essence that could last him years. He never saw the strange man with the bloody teeth again, but he remained grateful.

The child's stirring brought him back from his memories, and he grinned down at the boy as his eyes fluttered open.

When the boy's eyes focused in on Needlebone, he groaned.

The pale monster bowed low with mock gentility. "Welcome to Needlebone's kingdom, little rabbit."

The child strained against his bonds, but they didn't budge. He moaned with defeat and surveyed the room. "What are you going to do to me?"

Needlebone walked toward his worktable and held up part of the Apparatus. It resembled a feature-less metal mask, with several rubber tubes protruding from its slightly rusting surface. The five tubes were roughly the diameter of silver dollars: one over the mouth, two over the eyes, and one on each cheek. The tubes led from the mask to a metal box on the worktable. The box only had two features: a lever and a small spout. A large, empty jar sat beneath the spout.

Needlebone's grin grew even larger, and he stepped toward the child.

"The wounded little rabbit has run a merry race, but the race has ended. Now, Needlebone is famished. But don't worry, little rabbit will not be alone in Needlebone's pantry." He glanced at the cabinet of jars filled with red dust.

The child's eyes followed his and widened with terror—pleasing Needlebone. Fear made the essence more potent.

"No, wait!" The child strained hard against his bonds.

Needlebone noticed that the knot near the swollen hand seemed rather loose, but the restraints wouldn't be necessary much longer. He stood behind the boy and lifted the metal mask above his head.

"Goodnight, little rabbit. Dark dreams ahead."

"No, no, stop!"

The child pleaded and struggled vainly as the pale monster slipped the metal mask over his face and tightened the thick leather strap across the back of his head. The rusted metal and rubber contraption muffled the child's screams, but Needlebone could still hear his faint cries as he walked back toward the bench.

As he reached for the lever, he salivated.

# CHAPTER ELEVEN

Jack checked the stopwatch as he trekked up the stony path. According to the watch face, twelve hours, fifteen minutes, and twenty-three seconds remained. Though it took Jack almost twice that long to get to the Edge, he forced himself to believe that he could make it back more quickly, since he knew the way.

He didn't stop to consider all the things that could delay their return. Such worries were a waste of time.

As he marched, he paid attention to his surroundings: a mountainous and barren landscape with a jagged, rocky path that kept nearly tripping Jack. Eventually, he forced himself to slow down and be deliberate and balanced with his steps. Everything about the Hinderwood was dark and shrouded, but the shadows on Needlebone's side of the wall felt heavy, as if they bore down on Jack's sore shoulders. Several times, he considered removing the flashlight from the pack, but he didn't want to give away his position. Besides, his eyes gradually became accustomed to the dark.

After some time, he approached a steep hill that obscured the surrounding area. The hill, like most of the landscape he'd seen since passing through the ivory gate, was dotted with rough stones protruding from the barren ground like crooked teeth in a broken mouth. One stone particularly close to the narrow path caught Jack's eye. He stopped, leaned down, and saw words in a language he didn't recognize carved into the rock.

However, just below the script, another etching read, "1971-1982."

Jack stepped back and scanned the area again. He saw faint inscriptions on all the stones scattered throughout the desolate mountain.

A couple yards from the first stone, Jack saw one written in English. He squinted and read, "Oliver Potter. Son and Brother. 1893-1902."

Jack shuddered, then continued on his way.

When he crested the hill, he received a panoramic view of a dark hellscape: a valley with a single road running through the middle. Dozens of the jagged memorial stones lined the black fields on either side. Other than the occasional thorn-covered weed and one immense, dead oak tree on the far side of the valley, he saw no vegetation or sign of life.

Across from Jack, on the opposite peak, was a tall, narrow building constructed from the same rough stones that covered the bleak valley. Jack didn't start for the building right away, though—he was mesmerized by what lay beyond.

For a long moment, Jack's brain couldn't process what he saw. Beyond the valley and the strange building, a pillar of darkness created an unimaginably large wall. But then, it wasn't darkness—it was *nothing*, a void, an utter absence of anything.

Staring at the null space gave Jack a headache, but he also struggled to look away. He felt almost drawn to it, like a fly slowly fluttering into the deadly blue light of a bug zapper.

Ben called this place "The Edge." At the time, Jack wondered, "The Edge of what?"

Apparently, the answer was, "Of anything and everything."

But Jack forcibly tore his gaze from the void and focused on the building. He saw a wooden door at the base and two windows overlooking the valley, one near the top of the tower and one halfway down. To Jack, the windows suggested the tower contained at least two or three floors.

He smiled at this. Multiple floors meant multiple options for getting inside.

He scanned one last time for any sign of movement and, seeing none, ran down the hill toward the building.

As he sprinted between the irregular headstones, Jack glimpsed some of the names carved crudely into the rocks. Some names struck him as old-fashioned, names he'd see only in history books, like Ephraim and Evangeline. Others sounded surprisingly modern, like Xander and Astra.

Jack wondered how many lost spirits met final, terrible ends at the hands of Needlebone.

A sudden irregularity in his peripheral vision made him skid to a stop at the base of the hill. From his vantagepoint, he could see straight into the window on the second floor of the tower.

The occupant grinned with too many teeth and waved down at him.

When Jimmy first disappeared into William Porter's shed, the streaming light blinded Jack too much to get a good look at his brother's kidnapper. Jack briefly saw a pale hand with long fingers gripping his brother's ankle and not much else.

But even if that same hand weren't waving at him—even if he'd seen nothing at all—Jack would have recognized his brother's kidnapper based on reputation alone.

Everyone he met referred to the monster as the Needlebone Man, and appropriately so. Even from a distance, he looked impossibly tall and thin, with a slim and sinewy frame that radiated wiry, manic strength.

"Where is he?" Jack shouted, his voice echoing throughout the valley.

The pale figure's Cheshire grin grew. He reached down, then threw something out the window toward Jack.

Jack didn't flinch. The small, dark object fell several yards ahead of him, near a deep hole.

When he looked back up at the Needlebone Man, the specter gestured theatrically for Jack to move forward and inspect the projectile.

Jack kept an eye on the window and walked toward the hole, which looked freshly-dug. A large, rough stone stood at one end, though nothing had been carved into it. The hole was only a couple feet wide but at least six feet deep. When Jack saw the small, red object near the edge, his world turned upside down.

It was Jimmy's rabbit foot—and it was covered in blood.

A high-pitched ringing reverberated through Jack's skull. In the background, he heard a furious scream. Only when his throat felt like it would split into ribbons did he recognize the unhinged bellow of rage as his own.

In one fluid motion, he slipped the rifle off his back, slid the stock into his shoulder, and fired into the window.

The Needlebone Man was already moving when he raised the rifle, but Jack still saw a spray of blue blood hit the ledge of the window. He pulled back the bolt, ejected the spent bullet casing, and racked another round into the chamber.

The thin figure didn't reappear, but raspy laughter filled the air.

"You want to play in my kingdom? Meet some of my toys!"

Jack ignored the voice and made his way to the wooden door at the foot of the tower. He stopped when he heard rocks and dirt shifting. Turning, he raised the rifle defensively—and paused in spite of himself when he saw the source of the noise.

The ground beneath the rough-cut headstones churned violently, black dirt shifting and sinking as if air pockets were collapsing underground.

Amidst the rolling earth, the heads and limbs of children and younger teens clawed their way up from below the soil, climbing free from the desolate ground.

All the children were the sickly color of a fish's underbelly—as if they'd never seen the sun, as if they'd been completely drained of blood. Black earth covered their rotting clothes and emaciated frames. Where Jack could see intact faces, he saw strange scars on sunken cheeks and around slack-jawed mouths, the latter filled with rotting teeth.

All of them stared ahead, every eye socket empty.

Initially, they stood upright in front of the stones bearing their names—too many for Jack to count. Dozens, at least. But, as if triggered by some unseen command, all of them turned their eyeless gazes toward Jack.

A moment of deafening silence fell over Needle-bone's valley.

Then, all the reanimated children emitted a single, angry scream—and hurtled toward Jack.

Several gunshots echoed in rapid succession as three undead puppets close to Jack collapsed in a life-less heap. He racked in another round from the magazine, took a step forward, and shot the next through the chest. He watched to see if this would be effective, if headshots would be necessary, but the pale figure dropped, fragments of rib blown out his back.

Jack ejected the spent five-round magazine, pulled another from the side pocket of his backpack, and inserted it into the bottom of the rifle. He leapt behind the rock without an inscription and steadied the front of the rifle on the sturdy base.

The horde of lifeless bodies charged forward, but Jack dropped five more before they got within fifteen yards of him.

Jack reached for another magazine, but the weight felt wrong. It hadn't been loaded yet. He quickly checked the others, and they were all empty as well.

He'd only had time to load one spare with Ezekiel's special rounds.

Jack gritted his teeth angrily, then sighed, standing up to lean the rifle against the stone. When the backpack fell from his shoulders and thudded against the dark ground, he reached down into the special sleeve sewn into the pack.

The eldest Doe brother pulled the Heaven Breaker free.

The weight of the bat felt reassuring in his hand. He stretched his shoulder and took a slow, deliberate practice swing. The hand-carved ash whistled as it cut through the night air. Jack exhaled and stepped out from behind the rock.

Since coming to the Hinderwood, he'd suffered a beating from a gang of crow spirits, fled the attacks of dead coyotes, and encountered all manner of strangeness and difficulty. After all that, when he finally made it to the edge of the nightmare, Needlebone taunted him and showed him that he was too late.

The eldest Doe brother was an angry kid—and he needed to do something about all of it.

As the mass of dead bodies neared him, the carvings that Ezekiel added to his bat began to glow, emitting a light that reminded Jack of William Porter, of how his hands glowed when he fought to secure the shed door. The radiant carvings shone out sharply against the black ash of the bat.

Holding the glowing club, Jack Doe stepped into the middle of the path bisecting the valley, then dragged the heel of his boot in the dirt, creating a line. He took one step back from the line and brandished the bat in front of him, like a samurai staring down an oncoming adversary. Anyone close enough to watch the scene unfold would have been surprised to see that Jack's expression remained cool and calm.

He was still relaxed when he hit the lead undead assailant in the temple and sent him spinning into the rocky dirt. His face was still tranquil as he sidestepped one reanimated teenager and broke another's leg at the knee.

Unfortunately, the onslaught was just beginning. The mass of corpses surged around Jack like a grasping, gnashing wave of cracked fingernails and broken teeth.

He was not overwhelmed. Jack spun like a whirling Dervish—though, a rather violent one.

He swung the glowing bat in rapid, powerful arcs that lit up the dark, desolate valley like a light show, offsetting his attack with elbows, knees, and even headbutts. For the first time in his life, Jack didn't hold back. He brawled tooth and nail until his sinews were on fire. He fought through the occasional cold sting of the corpses' touch on his bare skin. Sweat soaked his clothes, making his grip on the bat slippery. Neverthe-less, pale, mud-covered corpses piled up in a half-circle surrounding Jack's line in the dirt.

He managed to thin the crowd of undead enemies, but he was still outnumbered. As the wall of bodies grew higher, many attackers began circling around the back, while the main onslaught threatened to overturn the pile of gore on top of Jack.

He tried to push back against the toppling wall while swinging at a tall, pale boy with a jaw that hung limply to one side. The jaw, along with the rest of the moving corpse's face, cracked sharply, and his tall form crumpled at Jack's feet. But as the body fell, a clawed hand grasped the eldest Doe brother by the sleeve of his jacket.

Jack wasn't expecting the sudden dead weight, and he stumbled.

As he fell to one knee, two more animated corpses sprang forward and knocked him flat. They clawed and gnashed at him, but he managed to shove the bat between his face and their teeth and keep them at bay. Pushing against the Heaven Breaker, he tried to create enough space between the two attackers to get to his feet—but he felt the almost four-foot-high stack of bodies begin to topple.

Shifting his grip so he braced the bat with one hand, he flicked his other fist out in a quick jab that struck one of the pale groping figures on the bridge of its nose. When the eyeless corpse slumped, Jack rolled to the side, pushing the suddenly-slack body on top of the other assailant.

He tried to get to his feet, but he was too late.

The barrage of animated cadavers knocked over the wall of bodies.

Before he could scramble away, Jack was buried beneath a stinking pile of rotting flesh and broken bones. The dead weight of the corpses knocked the wind out of him.

His grip on the bat slipped, and the Heaven Breaker was lost in the pile of rot.

The frenzied press of the still-animated dead children bore down on the pile. Jack tried to force his way out, but the weight was too much. Before long, they would reach him, and there was nothing he could do.

For a stretching, endless moment, Jack lay paralyzed—not only from the weight of the twice-dead above him, but from his own terror. He heard rotten skin being heaved and torn by the frenzied children, all forced into half-life by a monster.

Then, he heard metal swishing through the air, punctuated by a noise reminiscent of chopping meat. Jack didn't think the undead seemed coherent enough to use a weapon, so he wondered about the source of the commotion as he vainly struggled to free himself.

Some of the weight above him lifted. He wondered if Needlebone himself had arrived to finish him off.

At least he wouldn't be far behind Jimmy.

Jack heard the grunt of someone exerting themselves, and two bodies moved off his back. Wasting no time, he rolled over and raised his hands defensively.

214

But there was no reanimated corpse standing above him. Neither did he see the tall, grinning form of the Needlebone Man.

Instead, it was the ghost in the fox mask who stood above him on the pile of gore. His coat and mask were covered in blood, and he held a short dagger in one hand. In his other hand, he gripped the Heaven Breaker.

Jack braced himself. But the bat dropped harmlessly on the ground, near his own hand.

The eldest Doe brother stared up, carefully watching the spirit who pursued him across Limbo.

The masked ghost pointed toward the tower.

Jack looked up, and his breath caught in his throat.

Jimmy stood in the window. Jack saw his mouth moving, though he couldn't hear him.

Jack started to yell something back, but Jimmy was wrenched out of view by Needlebone's thin but powerful arm.

When Jack turned back to the spirit in the blood-stained fox mask, the ghost nodded at the bat and pointed at the tower.

The eldest Doe brother saw more of the dead coming for him and the fox ghost. He grabbed the Heaven Breaker and got to his feet.

Before Jack could even ask why the spirit helped him, the wiry ghost in the bloody fox mask leapt from the pile of corpses. He brandished the dagger and sprinted toward the oncoming barrage of undead.

Jack started toward the tower door, then stopped. He looked up at the tall, narrow building, and he thought for a moment. Finally, he hurried back to the uninscribed stone and picked up his backpack.

The ghost in the mask sifted through the attacking horde of the dead with an expert flurry of fierce slices.

Jack said a quick prayer for the strange spirit, then jogged toward the tower.

$$\Delta$$

While Needlebone focused on the commotion outside, Jimmy worked to escape.

First, he tugged on the restraints that bound him to the table, hoping something would pull free—and thankfully, the knot around his damaged hand seemed looser than the rest. After some more struggling, Jimmy managed to slip his wrist out of it.

Though the swelling in his hand made it difficult, Jimmy first removed the metal apparatus from his face, then untied the other cords. He moved quickly but quietly, determined to avoid Needlebone's attention.

When a bullet drove itself into the stone wall across from him, Needlebone moved away from the window, but he paid Jimmy no mind. The pale monster's eyes rolled back inside his head—he concentrated on something not visible, or not visible to Jimmy, at least.

The youngest Doe brother fully intended to use the opportunity to sneak away, but he hesitated. Though the machine's horrible mask muffled all sound, Jimmy knew he'd heard Needlebone yelling at *someone*.

And despite everything, Jimmy's thoughts immediately turned to his brother.

When he ran toward the window and looked out, a strange sight greeted him—even stranger than the other things he'd seen on his journey.

Jack stood with someone wearing a fox mask amidst dozens of mangled corpses.

The person in the mask pointed up at Jimmy.

When Jack looked up, Jimmy called out to his brother—just before Needlebone opened his eyes and jerked him off his feet.

Needlebone wrenched Jimmy abruptly away from the window, dislocating the boy's shoulder. Shards of pain exploded up his arm as the tall ghoul dragged him back to the makeshift operating table.

Jimmy lashed out at the tall cabinet full of jars as they passed, catching hold of one. The glass container was surprisingly heavy and warm. At his touch, the sand vibrated slightly and, to his surprise, gave off a vibrant red glow. Jimmy didn't waste time wondering—he hurled the jar at the back of Needlebone's head as hard as he could.

The glass shattered, several shards implanting in the back of Needlebone's head and neck. The monster winced, and his grip on Jimmy's wrist loosened for a moment.

Jimmy wrenched his arm free. The pain was so intense that he lost his equilibrium momentarily, and he thought he might vomit. Forcing the bile down, he hurried for the door.

As he ran, he glanced at his captor, hoping to find him seriously wounded.

Needlebone stood upright, seemingly unharmed —but he made no move toward Jimmy. He focused on the red sand freed from the jar.

The sand slowly lifted from the ground in a large mass, held together by fierce, red light.

Without moving, Needlebone stared at the sand, an expression of surprise warping his consistently sadistic face in an unnatural way.

The glowing sand swirled around the room in an expansive arc. Though the Needlebone Man lunged forward, grasping for it, the sand weaved to avoid his clutches.

The swirling mass paused, for just a moment—as if regarding Jimmy, Needlebone, and the room—and then, it flew out the window.

Jimmy didn't wait to see Needlebone's reaction. He ran through the open doorway to the winding stair-case, cradling his dislocated arm against his chest and taking the stairs two at a time. Every time he bounced, pain shot through his shoulder, and his swollen hand throbbed with a likely infection, but he didn't care. He was consumed by thoughts of escaping, of getting out, of reaching his brother.

If he could just get to Jack, everything would be okay.

"Rabbit! What have you done, little rabbit?"

Jimmy heard a thud behind him as the Needlebone Man emerged rapidly from the room.

Without stopping, Jimmy glanced behind and saw the pale, grinning ghoul lunging down the steps like an animal. He bared his thin, sharp teeth, and his face contorted in a mask of rage.

"You let it get away! Evil little rabbit!"

Jimmy reached the door. He tried to lift the beam barring his way and kick the door open in one smooth move, but the beam jammed in its track. As he pulled hard with his good arm, the heavy wooden barricade started sliding up and out.

Then, he was pulled off his feet and slammed hard into the wooden steps.

Jimmy tried to get up, but all his energy was spent. He was too tired, too hurt from all he'd endured. He tried to muster some last bit of strength, but Needlebone's horrible face leaned over him from above.

The monster's lips parted, revealing a sneering grin, and a string of saliva dripped down onto Jimmy's forehead. "Little rabbit never learns. No one escapes Needlebone." Then, he grabbed Jimmy's ankle and dragged him back up the stairs.

It took everything out of Jimmy just to keep his head from bouncing off the wooden steps. But as he lifted his head, he looked back at the door, hoping he'd at least knocked the bar loose enough for Jack to force his way inside the tower.

To his dismay, the heavy beam had fallen neatly back into its track.

Jimmy groaned hopelessly.

"Let him go."

Both Needlebone and Jimmy craned their heads to the top of the stairs.

Jack stood on the top step with an expression of cold fury. He held the Heaven Breaker in front of him, its glowing, carved runes illuminating the dark stairway.

Jimmy felt the monster's grip loosen, and his ankle fell free.

$$\Delta$$

Needlebone snarled ferociously. Without a word, and with supernatural quickness, Jimmy's captor bounded up the remaining steps—like a frog leaping through the black sludge of a swamp onto an unsuspecting insect.

Jack swung the bat, but Needlebone deftly slipped under the blow and tackled the eldest Doe brother back into the crude operating room, slamming the boy's shoulder against the corner of the wooden restraint table.

Needlebone raised a foot to stomp on Jack's chest, but he rolled away quickly, wincing. Then, Jack grabbed the Heaven Breaker again, delivering a sharp upward kick to Needlebone's knee cap.

As his attacker stumbled, Jack leapt to his feet.

He brought the bat down hard on Needlebone's extended arm, and the monster's wrist snapped with a vicious cracking noise.

Jack pivoted and swung the bat hard at his head, but the tall, thin figure slipped to the side of the blow with frightening speed.

Before the eldest Doe Brother could reorient, the wounded ghoul's good hand darted out and raked his fingernails down Jack's face. Blood ran from the cuts.

Jack kicked out at his attacker's groin, but the monster was too fast. He weaved to the side and back-handed Jack with a blow that seemed far too strong for his bony arms.

$$\Delta$$

Jimmy hobbled up the stairs to help, looking around for anything that would allow him to join the fight. When he saw Jack's grappling hook wedged into the corner of the tower window, he actually smiled. He'd gotten that for Jack as a Christmas present the previous year.

"Get out of here!" yelled Jack, feinting with the bat and delivering an elbow to the Needlebone Man's throat.

The monster staggered back with a gasp.

The eldest Doe brother took the opportunity, rushing forward and kneeing him in his emaciated stomach.

It felt wrong, just leaving—but Jimmy typically listened to Jack, especially in times of crisis. He forced himself to step backward and edge down the stairs.

$$\Delta$$

Needlebone roared and lunged for Jimmy. "No!"

But Jack caught the monster by the hand that hung limply from his broken wrist, and he held tight.

Grinding his teeth in pain, the monster whirled around ferociously. His good hand shot toward Jack like a bullet and grabbed him firmly by the neck. His long fingers curled around the boy's throat and pressed hard on his windpipe.

Jack didn't have enough leverage to swing the bat, so he rammed the handle into the side of the creature's head.

Needlebone winced, but he didn't loosen his grip.

Jack yanked hard on the broken wrist, simultaneously driving the handle of the bat into the monster's nose.

Finally, the monster's grip went slack, and Jack dropped to the floor.

"You aren't taking him," said Needlebone, his voice sounding hollow. He stared down at Jack with hatred. Looming over the eldest Doe brother, the thin ghoul seemed even taller than usual, with something spiderlike in his quick, sharp movements. His right hand still hung limply from a bent wrist, and blue blood trickled down the side of his face, but he didn't seem weary or hampered by his wounds.

As Jack watched, the broken wrist twitched and straightened. The blue trickle of blood slowed. Needle-bone radiated menace as he stepped forward, placing a foot on Jack's bat before the eldest Doe brother could lift it.

"But you can go first!" The Needlebone Man kicked Jack hard in the ribs.

The eldest Doe brother lost his breath and gasped for air. As he worked to keep his grip on the bat at all costs, his vision cleared, and he saw the monster reach down for his neck again.

Jack rolled backward quickly to create some space, and he used the bat to push himself up off the ground to a kneeling position.

When he found his feet again, he stared at the monster in front of him. The creature's injuries healed rapidly, and he didn't seem to be tiring. He was too fast to fight. Jack could feel himself tiring out. He knew he'd have to end this soon, or he'd be sunk.

With a quick breath, the eldest Doe brother charged forward. The Needlebone Man had been braced for another swing of the bat, but the lunge took him by surprise.

Still holding the Heaven Breaker, Jack hit him low and wrapped his arms around the creature's thin but powerful frame. He dug in with his shoulder—and he kept charging forward.

The Needlebone Man seemed to realize what he was doing at the last moment, but it was too late.

They both fell through the open window to the dark ground below.

# INTERLUDE SEVEN:
## SPECTATORS

William Porter tried to make Ms. Dubois as comfortable as possible, given that they were in a funeral parlor. She rested some before eventually sitting up again. Even then, the mortician thought she looked frailer by the minute.

Placing a glass of water beside the couch where she sat, he told her they would be right back, and she responded with nothing more than a silent nod. William Porter sighed and walked out the side door with Ceri.

When the door shut behind him, he examined his watch, did some quick math in his head, and groaned. He looked at his dog. "They're not going to make it."

Ceri stared at him.

"Maybe. It's risky though."

Ceri said nothing.

"Even if we did, there's no guarantee! We'd just be hoping it caused a distraction."

Ceri sat down and cocked her head.

William Porter sighed. "You heard the lady; the boys are resourceful. Maybe they can still figure it out."

Ceri waited.

William Porter stared at his dog for a long time. Then, he shook his head, cursed, and marched toward the old shack. "Alright then, I guess we're in for a fight."

Ceri followed close behind.

In front of the ramshackle building, William Porter stopped. The shed looked innocuous without the iron bar, ancient lock, and heavy-duty chain stretched across it. Over the years, William Porter memorized every square inch of the shack's walls. He saw the shed when he was awake, he saw it when he slept. It always lingered in the edges of his thoughts.

But he only ever opened the door a handful of times—most in the past forty-eight hours, to signal Jack Doe.

William Porter closed his eyes. He took a long, deep breath, filling his belly with oxygen and expelling it so deeply that it rattled his bones. Then, he opened his eyes and stretched his shoulders and back before looking over at his friend.

Ceri nuzzled against his leg once, then stepped in front of him and readied herself.

William Porter nodded. Then, he opened the door.

Light spilled out from the shed, fully illuminating William Porter's backyard. Wind rushed out and sent his hat hurtling into the distance. In the face of it all, the mortician stood firm, his hands at his sides, palms turned up. The symbols tattooed in his flesh glowed warmly.

A deep, primal growl started in the massive dog's belly before emerging as a warning roar, her mouth glowing with razor-sharp teeth.

Before long, shadowy figures appeared on the fringes of the light, as if peering out—checking to see if the coast was clear.

"Brothers and Sisters, I assure you, there is no peace for you out here," he said.

The shadows drew closer, more appearing behind them. The mortician's eyes narrowed.

"I will guarantee it."

For a moment, the shadowy spirits paused. Then, they burst from the shed.

The mortician and the dog stepped forward to meet them.

As two spirits hit him head-on, Porter growled, "I told you, we shouldn't have let that boy through the door!"

Ceri said nothing.

Δ

Three miles away, Buford and Cash sat in creaking rocking chairs on their front porch, staring at the field behind their house and sipping some of Cash's moonshine. After their tour in Vietnam, they came home and built that house on the hill—the highest point in Opossum Trot. It looked out on much of the small town, giving them an excellent view of the goings-on down there.

A slight chill hung in the dark night air. The bug zapper cast a blue glow on the porch, and occasionally, mosquitoes crackled as they flew into the deadly light.

The old men ignored their view of the town, however, focusing instead on a fox that ran through the tall grass in the field. The creature's orange fur stood out, even in the dark.

At one point, the fox pounced, then sat up with something small and wriggling hanging from its mouth. Rather than disappear with its prey, the graceful hunter sat still, staring back at Buford and Cash.

The old warriors said nothing—a rare feat for them.

The fox regarded them curiously, then turned and departed.

Suddenly, they heard a loud, rushing noise, like a semi-truck passing nearby. Both men turned and looked toward town.

A radiant white light created a blinding pillar on the far side of Main Street. A scream of air filled the town, and the other-worldly light intensified.

Buford and Cash stared blankly at the scene.

After several minutes of silence, Cash turned to Buford. He raised an accusing eyebrow.

"I told you, you shouldn't have given that boy a gun."

Δ

Ezekiel and Eleanor Blacklock sat in their living room, a rare and quiet moment for the couple. All their guests had retired for the night or otherwise occupied themselves. Even Chester fell asleep earlier, snug in his small dog bed in the corner.

The Blacklocks embraced the opportunity and decided to be couch potatoes. Ezekiel watched television, and Eleanor curled up beside him to read a book.

Suddenly, a piercing scream rang from the attic.

The Blacklocks shared a confused look. Ms. Abigail spent years crying and moaning in the late hours of the night, but for the past few years, her cries became rarer and rarer. And she'd never screamed like this.

Before either could comment, a heavy thud reverberated from deep within the basement of the boarding house. The Blacklocks turned toward the hallway, staring at a rather ordinary-looking antique grandfather clock.

Another thud rumbled from the depths of the house, as if an insane monster were throwing itself against the walls of an ancient cage. They waited for another thud, but instead, they were inundated with an inhuman screech that made both of them wince.

Eleanor turned back to her husband.

"I told you, you shouldn't have given that boy bullets."

# CHAPTER TWELVE

The second-floor window of the tower was not overly high off the ground, and Jack managed to land on top of Needlebone, but the impact of the fall still knocked the wind out of him.

A rotten scent hung on the pale monster, and a greasy film covered his skin. Jack gagged to be near him, but he forced himself to reach for the ghoul's throat.

Before Jack could get a grip, the Needlebone Man hit him with the heel of his palm, seemingly unfazed by their fall.

The blow sent Jack sprawling backward. He hit his head on a rock, and as his vision blurred, a large hand grabbed the back of his collar. He felt himself being dragged down the hill—toward the void at the edge of the valley. The cliff dropped endlessly off into the strange abyss.

Jack's head lolled to the side, and he glanced down, surprised to see the Heaven Breaker still clenched in his fist. Dizzy as he was, he rolled over onto his belly facing Needlebone. He lashed out blindly with the bat but hit only empty space.

Releasing his collar, Needlebone kicked Jack in the ribs with a foot that felt like a sledgehammer.

Jack groaned and tried to climb to his feet, but another stomp sent him back into the dirt. Even without looking up, he sensed the Needlebone Man's grin.

The raspy, mocking voice croaked, "Has the dog tired of barking and biting?"

"Kill you…" Jack muttered, breathlessly.

"No, you will burn in the dark, until even your memory has faded into nothing."

Jack heard a loud crack, and the Needlebone Man flew back into a nearby stone. Blue blood trickled from his side and mouth, and he looked momentarily dazed.

Jack flopped over and raised his head.

Jimmy stood a couple yards away holding Buford's rifle. He steadied the gun against a memorial stone to fire, but his dislocated shoulder hindered his effort to reload.

Pushing up from the stone, the Needlebone Man stalked forward.

When Needlebone reached him, Jimmy gave up on the reload and swung the butt of the rifle. But Needlebone ducked under the gun easily and grabbed the youngest Doe brother.

After lifting Jimmy off his feet, Needlebone hurled him down the hill toward the edge of the cliff. The rifle fell from Jimmy's grip and rolled away into the dirt.

Jack gasped and tightened his grip on the bat. With a deep breath, he forced himself to rise to one knee.

The pale monster glanced at Jack, grinned, and hurtled down the hill after Jimmy.

"Wait!" Jack yelled.

The Needlebone Man hit Jimmy at a run, and they both disappeared over the edge of the cliff.

Jack screamed and ran forward. As he approached the Edge, he saw nothing—only the cliff and the colorless oblivion beyond. Cold sweat trickled down his blood-stained face, but he ran to the spot where Jimmy disappeared, then leaned over.

An oversized hand shot up and grabbed him by the collar, yanking Jack off his feet.

He landed hard, more than six feet down, on a stone cliff emerging from the side of the rock face. Jack almost rolled over the side of the narrow outcropping, but his hand shot out, catching the Heaven Breaker before it rolled into the void.

"Careful playing fetch, Fido." The Needlebone Man loomed over him from the other side of the out-cropping.

Behind him, Jimmy sat on the ground, his back against the face of the cliff and his eyes half closed. He didn't seem to register Jack at all.

The pale monster chuckled softly and spread his arms. Though his broken wrist had healed entirely, dark lines of dried blood trailed from his head to his chest, and glass still protruded from the side of his head.

"Swing away, dog," he laughed.

Jack got to his feet. He wiped his brow and exhaled softly. He stared at the Needlebone Man for a moment, then shook his head. "Just let us go."

"There's nowhere to go." The Needlebone Man cocked his head curiously, as if Jack fundamentally misunderstood the simplest, clearest truth. "This is my world. Dogs, rabbits, it's all the same to me. You're all just food."

Jack stared at the monster, then he looked at his brother. He saw the wound on his hand, the bruises everywhere, the strange marks on his face. Thinking of the bloody rabbit's foot, he looked back hard at the Needlebone Man.

His right fist tightened around the bat until his knuckles were white.

His head turned slightly, his jaw clenched, and his eyes narrowed.

Behind the Needlebone Man, Jimmy smiled.

Jack raised the bat. He wasn't fast enough to hit the monster, but his brother had been put through Hell, and he meant to go down swinging for it.

The Needlebone Man prepared to dodge the blow and push Jack over the Edge.

Neither saw Jimmy fall forward.

The youngest Doe brother grabbed the Needle-bone Man's ankles and wrapped his arms around them, holding them fast with all his remaining strength.

The monster looked down in surprise.

And Jack swung the Heaven Breaker as hard as he could.

Light radiated from the bat, cutting a vicious arc through the darkness before crashing into Needle-bone's skull.

The Needlebone Man's head cracked to the side and his eyes rolled backward. He stumbled sharply, his legs shaking.

Jimmy released his ankles and rolled away.

Roaring, Jack launched into a brutal flurry of blows, forcing the monster back until his large, white frame perched on the edge of the cliff. Jack paused only a moment and stared into the Needlebone Man's eyes.

At the edge of Needlebone's hate and mania and fury, Jack saw a glimmer of fear.

But he swung the bat a final time. The hardwood slammed into the monster's ribs, sending him careening over the Edge.

Jack fell to one knee and sighed heavily. He waited a second, then stood up, turned, and walked toward Jimmy. But his brother stared at something behind him, and he heard overgrown fingernails scratching on stone.

Turning around, Jack saw the long-fingered white hand clutching the edge. The monster hung off the side of the cliff with one arm while the other dangled uselessly, crooked and shattered from the recent barrage of blows. Blue blood splattered down his neck and chest, and his head hung limply to one side. His slack-jawed mouth displayed broken, jagged teeth.

As Jack stared, the monster slowly raised his head and stared back. His eyes were cloudy but worked hard to focus.

"It's not fair," wheezed the monster, softly.

Jack just stared.

"I claimed him! He was mine!" The monster's voice turned sorrowful, almost pleading. "You shouldn't have come here."

"He's my brother," said Jack.

The Needlebone Man stared, not comprehending.

"I'm always going to come for him."

The monster's eyes cleared for a brief and harrowing moment. "No one came for me."

Jack regarded the monster.

Then, the Needlebone Man sighed, closed his eyes, and let go.

He fell, surprisingly slowly, into the all-encompassing nothingness—fading into the void until nothing remained.

"Jack."

Jack turned toward his brother. The youngest Doe sat against the side of the rock face again, looking almost as pale as the Needlebone Man, one of his hands swollen with infection.

Jack knelt down beside him and placed a hand on his shoulder. "You look terrible."

"You smell worse," Jimmy replied with a grin.

"Well, we could both do with soap and water," Jack agreed. "I call the shower when we get back."

"I just need to rest first." Jimmy's eyes fluttered.

"Sorry, kid. We've got to hit the road. Come on, I'll boost you up." Jack looked at the cliff face. He thought he could scale it, but he'd have to get Jimmy up first.

His brother nodded and got unsteadily to his feet, his lips trembling.

Jack held his hands together for Jimmy to step into, but when his little brother moved forward, he stumbled. Jack had to catch him to keep him from falling.

"I can't, Jack, I'm too tired," said Jimmy, struggling to stay upright even with his brother steadying him.

"Here, just try to catch the edge." Jack gritted his teeth and lifted Jimmy. He took a breath, strained, and pressed his brother's shaking frame above his head. He held the weight as long as he could, and he felt Jimmy reaching, but it wasn't working.

His little brother gasped, "I can't do it."

Jack lowered Jimmy and set him gently on the ground.

"I'm sorry," whispered the youngest Doe brother.

"Don't apologize," the eldest replied.

Jack turned around and reached into one of the inner pockets of his coat. He produced the antique stopwatch the mortician gave him two days earlier, though it felt like years.

Only two hours remained.

Jack sighed and shook his head.

"What's that?" asked Jimmy, glancing over.

Jack tossed the watch off the side of the cliff. "Nothing."

Then, Jack sat down beside his brother. He tried to pray, like Ms. Dubois would have wanted, but softly—so Jimmy wouldn't hear him and worry.

## Δ

After a few minutes, the Doe brothers heard boots approaching from above them on the rocky soil. Jack instinctively reached for the bat, and both brothers looked up.

An orange fox mask leaned over the edge.

Jimmy raised an eyebrow.

Jack gritted his teeth and stood up. "What do you want?" he asked, angrily.

The ghost in the mask said nothing.

"Answer me! You've followed me across the whole underworld, even helped me in that fight. Why? What do you want? Who are you?"

The fox sat down on the edge, so his feet hung out above the Doe brothers. He stared down at them for a moment, then raised his hands. Jack tensed, but they were empty; the knife he'd used in the fight hung harmlessly from his belt.

The quiet spirit touched the sides of his face and lifted his mask.

Jack heard Jimmy's breath catch in surprise while his own face widened in shock. They both stared at the boy: older than Jimmy, but a little younger than Jack. Except for his red hair, he looked just like the Doe brothers—though, perhaps, a bit paler.

He stared solemnly at them, waiting.

Jack felt Jimmy tug on his jacket, heard him ask something, but he couldn't make out the words. He couldn't look away from the ghost sitting above him or from the brilliant white glow slowly building around them.

Like a sluggish explosion or a lumbering monster, the light from his Nightmare bore down on them, as if finally surrounding long-sought prey. Jack closed his eyes, but he could no longer avoid the light.

So, he braced himself and let the monster finally overtake him.

$$\Delta$$

Jack watched from above as three brothers dressed up in their Halloween costumes—though, they weren't really full costumes, he supposed. The middle brother only managed to scrounge up a few simple masks. All were made of plastic and obscured the entire face. Even the eyes were painted on, with vision only possible through small slits above the cheeks.

The eldest brother took the dog mask: the one with pointed ears, a lupine snout, a canine tooth slipping past hungry lips, and a set of intense yellow eyes.

The youngest brother, no more than four, picked up the rabbit mask with long ears and whiskers.

The middle brother, who deftly procured the masks from the drug store—sans payment—chose the fox disguise that remained.

He'd gotten the masks after they escaped from their group home. The middle brother was gifted at finding ways in and out of places, and escape became necessary when they realized Halloween activities wouldn't be permitted that year. The family would certainly kick them out when they returned, but it didn't matter.

Halloween was the brothers' favorite holiday, and it could not be missed.

The eldest brother heard about a rich neighborhood several blocks away that gave out full-sized candy bars and caramel apples. Unfortunately, they ran late getting started, and the neighborhood would be a long walk on foot. They decided to cut through an industrial park. The youngest brother feared the large, aluminum buildings and the dark, monstrous silhouettes of the machinery, but the eldest brother reassured him that the shortcut wouldn't take long.

They made their way through the park quickly enough, but as they crawled through a hole in the chain-link fence surrounding the industrial sites, the middle brother suddenly flinched. He raised the fox mask slightly, then heard the unmistakable approach of footsteps.

The eldest brother raised his mask and scanned the fence line. The full moon and clear sky lit the area just enough for him to see a man walking quickly toward them.

The eldest brother scooped up the youngest, and he and the middle brother bolted toward the woods. They both heard the man hurrying after them, yelling something in a hoarse voice.

As they got closer, the woods turned out to be a thin strip of trees bordering a railroad track. The brothers were so concerned with the stranger pursuing them, that they didn't notice the approaching train.

The eldest glanced back at their pursuer. He was big and dirty, like he hadn't bathed or lived indoors in some time. They ran through the trees toward the rail line.

The rumble of the approaching train drew closer and closer. The light from the front car illuminated the scene.

The eldest held the youngest tightly and hurtled across the tracks. Heavy stones bordered the rail and lined the steep hill on the other side. Halfway down the hill, the pair skidded to a halt.

They glanced around, waiting for their brother to land beside them, but nothing happened.

The eldest set the youngest on his feet and gestured for him to wait; then, he hurried back up the hill. When he crested the top, his breath caught in his throat.

The middle brother crouched in the middle of the train track, pulling frantically on his leg. His foot had gotten wedged beneath a gap in the rail.

The train hurtled forward without slowing, white light covering everything and making it hard for the eldest brother to see.

He rushed forward, nonetheless.

Though he struggled with his brother's leg, trying to pull it free from the gap in the track, nothing budged. He gritted his teeth, wrenched the leg, and twisted hard—despite the moan of pain that escaped the fox mask. Still, the middle brother remained stuck, the blinding, screaming light bearing down on them both.

A small hand gripped the eldest brother's shoulder. The boy froze momentarily, staring into the fox's painted eyes.

The fox mask shook slowly back and forth.

The eldest brother said nothing.

Suddenly, the hand released his shoulder and pushed him hard in the chest.

As he fell backward down the hill, ten thousand tons of metal wreathed in blinding, electric light hit his brother at full speed.

The eldest brother screamed, and he fell blindly into the dark, only vaguely aware of the sudden sharp pain in his head as his skull cracked against a rock.

As he faded into unconsciousness, he knew only screaming and darkness.

Δ

"Jason," said Jack, softly.

The red-haired boy nodded, the corners of his mouth turning slightly up.

Jimmy looked back and forth between the two. His eyes rested on his eldest brother. "But how? I don't remember…"

"You were so little," said Jack.

"What about you?" asked Jimmy.

"The accident, it must have made me forget." He stared up at the familiar face in disbelief. "I'm sorry."

The red-headed boy didn't reply. Nothing needed to be said with words.

Instead, the middle Doe brother knelt down. With one hand, he anchored himself against the stone, and with his other, he reached over the edge of the cliff.

Because a brother evens the odds.

Jack picked up Jimmy and hoisted him over his head. Jason reached down and caught the youngest Doe brother's arm, and the weight lifted from Jack's shoulders as his younger brother pulled his youngest brother to safety.

Once Jimmy stood above him, supported in part by Jason, Jack tossed the Heaven Breaker up—then jumped, caught the edge of the cliff, and pulled himself over the side.

Jack and Jason supported Jimmy, and together, they all walked away from the Edge.

$$\Delta$$

The Doe brothers ascended the steep hill that led away from Needlebone's lair, away from the piles of newly-lifeless bodies—and Jack didn't have the heart to tell Jimmy they'd never manage the long trek in the few minutes remaining to them.

Even from the Edge, Jack saw the light to the east; though, not the quick blink William Porter had been using to signal him. The light shone constantly. And yet, it didn't matter. They had no time left to reach it.

They continued to trudge forward until Jimmy stopped in front of a large, gnarled tree Jack passed on his way into the valley.

"What are you—?" Jack began to ask, but Jimmy ignored him.

He stumbled forward and held his wounded hand out toward the tree, unwrapping the bloody cloth with a wince. Then, he wiped his swollen, blood-covered palm across the gnarled, wooden mouth of the tree.

Jack and Jason stared as the lips parted, revealing a gaping, man-sized mouth with jagged wooden teeth.

"What is this, Jimmy?" asked Jack.

"It's like a portal," Jimmy replied. "It's how he brought me here."

Jimmy led them into the dark, damp path inside the tree, sighing in relief when he saw a wall inscribed with symbols and etchings. Then, he stopped. "I don't know which one goes to Mr. Porter's."

The brothers scanned the wooden tapestry. Dozens of symbols wove in a web of ancient illustrations. Focusing on a single picture proved difficult, like playing a complex game of I-Spy on an intricate woodcut.

Jack's eyes finally homed in on a drawing near the ground: a large dog with pointy ears that stood between two tombstones. He tapped his youngest brother's shoulder and pointed.

Jimmy nodded and rubbed his bloody palm on the picture. All three brothers felt the tree shift slightly as the mural gave way to a new path.

Jack and Jason once again supported their younger brother, and together, they all walked down the dark road.

$$\Delta$$

William Porter hurled a struggling, shadowy form back into the shed and quickly glanced at his wristwatch. When he saw the time, he groaned, and not from the burning ache in his ancient muscles.

To his left, Ceri pounced on two shadow forms and tore into them with glowing teeth. Together, they managed to keep any spirits from progressing more than a couple yards from the gate—but only barely.

Three phantoms made of churning darkness rushed from the glowing doorway. William Porter spread his glowing palms, wrapped all three fleeing spirits in a tight bear hug, then dug in with his heels. His muscles strained, and he pushed all three dead fugitives back through the door.

With the spirits dispatched, he doubled over, his hands braced on his knees, and he heaved.

Ceri looked up in concern.

The shadow she'd been chewing used the opportunity to crawl back into the safety of the spirit world.

William Porter groaned and stood up straight. He stared at his dog for a moment, then looked at the glowing doorway. He looked back at his dog and nodded. "Okay. Do it."

Ceri cocked her head to one side and made a short, whining noise.

"There's no time. Go!" ordered William Porter.

Ceri stared for a beat longer, then turned and bounded into the shed. The giant, black dog split the white light as her dark, muscular frame dove into the blinding void. As she passed, William Porter thought she looked like a black hole imploding in a dying sun.

The mortician whispered a soft prayer in a dead language for his friend, then reached toward something on the ground. When he stood up, he held a wood-handled shovel in his grip. On the blade, a complex pattern of engraved symbols shone with brilliant white light, even in the presence of the open gate.

William Porter held the shovel with the blade up and across his chest, like a soldier marching with his rifle. He planted his feet in front of the glowing shed and waited.

Nothing happened for a moment.

Suddenly, several dark forms charged from the blinding light en masse. They knocked him backward, his heels cutting small trenches in the dirt, but he braced against the oncoming horde with the shovel handle. The mortician half-growled, half-groaned as he pressed back against the shadowy mob.

One spirit moved too close to the glowing head of the gardening tool and suddenly hissed, beginning to dissolve as if doused in acid.

Seizing his opportunity, William Porter stepped to the side of the churning mass of phantoms, delivering thundering blows with his luminous shovel.

The assault on the group of escaped spirits so consumed the mortician, that he didn't notice the white-gloved hand emerging from the shed or embracing the wooden door frame. He remained unaware when an immaculate, leather Oxford shoe stepped onto the wet grass. And just as he was forcing three screaming wraiths back to the gate, a well-dressed man with a bloody grin surfaced from the light—then vanished entirely.

William Porter kept fighting and hoped it wasn't in vain.

Δ

The brothers stepped out of the tree, and up ahead, Jack saw the barren town where he fought the crows in the burlap masks. His gaze did not linger on the empty, cobblestone street, however—the pillar of light radiating from William Porter's shed drew his attention. The beacon illuminated the entire forest, lighting the way to the shed.

"Come on," said Jack. He and Jason supported Jimmy's weight and hurried forward through the trees.

Eventually, he saw the familiar shape of William Porter's house—or, its dilapidated doppelganger, at least. But something stopped him in his tracks.

Dozens of spirits surrounded the house.

Some spirits looked indistinguishable from regular people, albeit with somewhat dated clothes. Many looked far stranger: sporting crude masks like the crows, unusually long limbs, or even glowing eyes. One spirit near the front porch opened his mouth, and a tiny, black hand reached out, grasping at the air erratically.

All the spirits clustered around the door frame, fighting and jostling for position as they tried to force their way through the door and the brilliant pillar of light.

Some near the back turned toward the Doe brothers when they approached.

Jack and Jason eased Jimmy down to support himself, and then, they reached for their weapons.

Suddenly, heavy breathing washed over the Doe brothers and all the assembled spirits. Every head turned sharply toward the woods opposite the house.

A feeling of surprisingly sharp panic hit Jack like a stun gun, nearly knocking him off his feet.

Next to him, Jimmy fell to the ground trying to crawl away. Jason searched frantically in every direction, as if for an escape route.

When he looked back toward the woods, Jack saw something big emerge from the oak trees. "What is that?" he asked.

Jimmy groaned from the ground.

"What?" Jack asked again.

Jimmy shook, struggling to speak, but managed, "That's the only thing in this place that scared Needlebone…"

A vaguely humanoid shape with too-long arms, skin the color and consistency of crude oil, and sharp, pointed spikes for hands loomed in the trees, standing over nine feet tall. A gray vapor hung in a cloud around the monster, following it as it slowly and methodically approached the mass of spirits.

When the gray mist neared Jack, terror overwhelmed him—as if it radiated from the horrifying shape—and the eldest Doe brother felt the intense urge to *flee*.

But Jack fought it. "No time. There's no time. There's no time," he said, forcing himself to repeat it. Wincing, he reached down and grabbed Jimmy's collar. As he pulled his youngest brother to his feet, he steadied Jason with his other hand. "We have to go forward," he croaked, lips trembling.

The other spirits scattered in every direction, abandoning their gambits to fight through the door. All around the Doe brothers, ghosts disappeared into the woods.

The path to the glowing doorway cleared except for the immense creature surrounded in the poisonous gray fog. The monster stood with its back to the glowing pillar, blocking the Does' way out of the Hinderwood.

Jack faced the dark, inky mass and took a defiant step forward. It took everything to keep from running in the opposite direction.

The monster advanced, its slick, black head devoid of all features except one: a lipless mouth, filled with row after row of short, jagged teeth, permanently bared. They sprung out of enflamed red gums, all lit horribly by the brilliant light of the door.

Without any other source for its senses, the monster's horrifying maw stared hungrily out at the Doe brothers—noticing them for the first time.

## Δ

The ancient being stared hungrily at the children. Two of the three were alive, and it had not tasted a living spirit in a long time. Though the nearby gateway tempted him, it could wait.

Hunger always came first to the monster known as the Pursuer.

Besides, the children offered him a pleasant surprise—the tallest one tried to withstand him.

*Everything* ran before the Pursuer.

When the monster focused its efforts on the noncompliant one, all three collapsed. The dead one and the small one tried to claw away from the Pursuer, but the tallest caught both by their jackets and held them in place. He covered the smaller two with his body and tried to crawl forward.

The Pursuer's patience ran out. It stepped closer, raising one of its long, sharp arms high above its head.

Then, a shadow fell over the monster's shoulders.

As the creature turned, something large leapt from the pillar of light, and—for the first time in hundreds of years—when impossibly powerful jaws closed around its neck, the monster knew what it was to be afraid.

The black dog's thunderous snarl echoed every enraged predator that ever emerged from darkness to call for blood. Her muscular frame bore down on the monster like a hurricane of claws and teeth.

For eons, the Pursuer feasted only on terrified prey seeking any blind escape. It felt unprepared for true combat.

When the massive dog tore chunks out of the Pursuer's dark flesh with her glowing teeth, the creature flailed wildly, screeched deafeningly, and tried to encircle the beast with one of its sharp tentacle arms.

Δ

Ceri caught the tentacle in her mouth and yanked the monster down into the dirt.

$$\Delta$$

As William Porter's dog battled the monster, Jack felt the all-encompassing horror dissipate. He figured Ceri took the creature's power out of commission. As if to confirm his suspicion, a couple spirits took their chance to dart from the woods and into the light of the open gateway.

The panic fled Jason and Jimmy's faces as well.

Jack's youngest brother stared in bewilderment at the violent struggle unfolding before them. "Not the weirdest thing I've seen in the past two days... but still."

"Go through the door," Jack ordered.

"What about—?" he started to ask, but Jack shoved him forward.

"Now!"

Jimmy stumbled forward, giving the monster and the giant dog a wide berth. When he reached the door frame, he caught hold of it to steady himself. Then, he flinched backward, dodging several spirits who hurtled through the shed door to retreat into the woods.

After a moment of recovery, Jimmy started to step through—but paused when Jack and Jason didn't follow.

"You're coming, right? Both of you?" he asked.

"Right behind you," Jack said softly.

Jason smiled and gave his younger brother a quick hug.

Jimmy held the embrace for a moment, then stepped into the light.

Jack turned back to Jason as the monster screeched in pain behind him. He stared into that pair of eyes that matched his and Jimmy's. "Could you? Come with us, I mean."

Jason shrugged as if he didn't know, but the question wasn't relevant.

Behind them, with a final, angry shriek, the Pursuer gave up and skittered away into the shadows.

Ceri watched it flee with a stoic expression, then walked toward the brothers. The black dog nudged Jack softly and stared pointedly at the glowing doorway.

Jack ignored her. "I didn't come here to leave a brother behind."

Jason shook his head, but Jack put a hand on his shoulder.

"I can't—" Jack stopped and swallowed hard. "Jason, I'm so sorry. I didn't…"

Jason wrapped his brother in a fierce hug.

The eldest Doe brother sighed, and an immense weight drifted away, just as he became aware of it. He hugged Jason back.

His younger brother whispered, "You never stopped being my big brother."

Then, Jason pushed him again—and Jack fell backward through the gateway. His hand shot out, grasping, but the middle Doe brother smoothly slipped out of his reach.

The last thing he saw as the light enveloped him was Jason, smiling and nodding. Then, he slid the fox mask back into place.

Jack yelled in protest, in grief.

But then he landed on the damp grass outside William Porter's shed.

Jimmy stared expectantly at the gateway, waiting. "Where's Jason?" he asked.

Jack looked at his brother.

"Jack, where's Jason?"

And for the first time in his memory, Jack openly cried.

# CHAPTER THIRTEEN

Jack and Jimmy sat in a hospital room in silence. Jack sported some new stitches, but otherwise, remained mostly intact.

His brother was another story. Jimmy's IV followed him on a rolling stand, several stitches decorated his body, and a sling hugged his arm to his chest, cradling a heavily bandaged hand. His hospital room was next door, but he hadn't spent much time in it. Though he'd come frighteningly close to losing the hand, neither of them felt particularly concerned about it at that moment.

The Doe brothers sat in plastic chairs beside Ms. Dubois's hospital bed.

Buford, Cash, and William Porter stood outside the room, talking in low voices.

"You boys need to rest," said Ms. Dubois, softly.

"We're fine, Ms. Dubois," said Jack.

"Don't lie to me, boy."

"Sorry."

She hadn't been alert much over the two days they'd been back. But at least one of the Doe brothers had been in her room the entire time. Jack even waited until Jimmy was coherent enough to sit with her before allowing the doctors to examine him.

"Well, since we're all awake anyways, there's something I need to tell you both." She nodded slightly toward her leather handbag on a table in the corner. "Jack, I've got some documents in there."

Jack walked across the room and opened the large bag, more of a satchel than a purse. Over the years, it held candy, gifts, Band-Aids, and some of the worst-but-well-intentioned cookies in the history of Opossum Trot. That night, the bag contained a manila folder thick with important-looking documents. Jack removed the papers and studied them.

"What are they?" asked Jimmy, craning his neck to see.

"Our records..." Jack scanned medical docu-ments, DHS reports, and more, all outlining almost everything that befell the brothers prior to coming to Opossum Trot—including the death of Jason Doe.

He looked up at Ms. Dubois in confusion. "You knew... But why?"

"Whenever they agreed to let me foster you boys, they gave me your full cases. But your caseworker said I shouldn't tell you about your other brother."

"Why?"

"She said you would remember in time, as part of your process. It was best to let you get there on your own. And besides, Jimmy was too young to remember anyways."

"You lied to us."

"I never lied to you." Ms. Dubois supported herself and met Jack's gaze firmly. She seemed like her old self for a moment. "You two may think you're tough, and I'll admit you have been through quite an ordeal, but I believe every child should get to be a kid. I was just trying to give you part of your childhoods back. I knew you would eventually remember and overcome it, but you needed time and a safe home. That's all I wanted."

Jack and Jimmy didn't reply.

Ms. Dubois slumped back slowly into her reclined hospital bed. Eventually, she asked, "Do you boys hate me?"

Jack and Jimmy moved remarkably fast for children who'd fought their way through the underworld two days prior. Before Ms. Dubois could blink, the Doe brothers came to her side and hugged her with gentle ferocity.

Jack broke the silence first. "You saved us. We owe you everything," he whispered.

"We could never hate you," Jimmy agreed, firmly.

Ms. Dubois hugged them back as best she could and gently patted each of them on the hand. "You two are good boys. I'm so proud of you both. Now, I just need to close my eyes for a minute."

She smiled at the Doe brothers—but it was a tight smile, and they could tell she was in a lot of pain. As they watched, she closed her eyes and began to doze off.

Jack and Jimmy returned to their uncomfortable plastic chairs and waited. After a few minutes, the door opened. Jimmy had been drifting off himself, and he flinched at the sound of the hinges squeaking. Jack stared at their new visitor.

He seemed familiar, but Jack couldn't say how.

"Good afternoon, gentlemen. You must be Jackson and James Doe. Is that correct?"

Though impossible to discern his age, the pale man dressed impeccably in a crisp, black suit, polished Oxford dress shoes, a white shirt, and a thin red tie with a silver pin shaped like a wing. His dark hair mirrored his suit with a sharp, neat part—potentially formed with a laser. He was tall, thin, and bespectacled, with a stern and serious expression. He carried a black leather briefcase, which he quickly opened, producing a clipboard and papers that he regarded carefully.

Jack had spent enough time in the foster care system to recognize a high-level government employee when he saw one. Nudging Jimmy softly, he warned him without a word to be on his guard. Then, Jack steeled himself.

"Yes, sir."

The man in the dark suit produced a pen and made a mark on his clipboard. He then raised his head and looked at Ms. Dubois, who slept soundly in her hospital bed.

"Then, this is Renee Dubois?" he asked.

"Yes," said Jack, warily.

He expected the man to make another mark on his clipboard, but he didn't. Instead, the strange bureaucrat did something peculiar: he stared at Ms. Dubois for several seconds. His expression softened, albeit slightly, and he closed his eyes. Softly, but deliberately, he exhaled—and something in the room seemed to change.

Before Jack could articulate that change, the man resumed his serious expression and turned back to the boys. "Young men, we need to discuss your future."

"So, you're the new case worker?" Jimmy asked.

"In a manner of speaking," he replied. "Now, in light of Ms. Dubois's decline in health, you will both require new living arrangements."

Jimmy started to protest, but Jack put a hand on his shoulder. "Ms. Dubois is too sick. She can't take care of us anymore," he explained. "And I'm still too young to take care of us on our own. There's no way they'll let us stay with her." Then, Jack turned to the man in the suit. "But we aren't leaving Opossum Trot."

The man regarded Jack—steadily, waiting.

"This place is our home. We have people who care about us and people we care about. Besides, we aren't leaving Ms. Dubois," Jack continued.

"You have to find someone here," Jimmy agreed.

"Or we'll just run off and come back, again and again, until I'm eighteen," said Jack, firmly.

"I do not believe it wise for the two of you to leave this town," said the neat man.

The Doe brothers raised their eyebrows in surprise. Caseworkers never agreed with them.

"You have both done well in this place, and, in light of the past forty-eight hours and its events, I believe it would be ill-advised for the two of you to stray far from the site in question."

"What does that mean?" asked Jack.

"Mr. William Porter has agreed to take you both into his care. These accommodations will allow you to remain in this town. I assume this would be amenable to you both?"

"What?" Jack repeated, disbelieving.

"We'd live with William Porter?" said Jimmy, in a similar tone.

"Yes," replied the caseworker, reviewing some papers on his clipboard. "You would be expected to assist with some of his responsibilities, but you would both be able to pursue any desired extracurricular activities. These extracurricular activities may include working for Buford McKinnon and Holt 'Cash' Freeman, running track, playing baseball, or whatsoever you should choose."

Jack could only say, "Wow."

"His house seems kind of creepy," noted Jimmy.

The neatly-dressed man stared at Jimmy for two beats, then said, "I am sure measures could be taken to make the space more comfortable."

The boys sat pondering in silence.

The man waited for a moment, then put his clipboard and papers back into his briefcase. He gave one last glance in Ms. Dubois's direction, which seemed almost reverential to Jack, then turned toward the door. "Rest assured, arrangements will be made. If there is nothing else, I must be on my way."

Jack took a step toward him. "It was wrong, keeping our brother's death from us."

The man slowly but deliberately turned, straightening his glasses as he regarded Jack. "Why?"

"I know the state probably thought it was 'best' for us," Jack said, making finger quotes. "But we went on like he wasn't even our brother anymore, and that's not right. It wasn't your choice to make."

The neat man in the dark suit met Jack's angry gaze firmly—but also thoughtfully, and without malice. "No, Mr. Doe, it was not my choice to make. But may I offer up something for your consideration?" His gaze traveled briefly to Ms. Dubois, then returned to Jack. "You are angry at yourself. You feel that by blocking out your brother, even as a side effect of trauma, you betrayed and lost him."

Jack looked away and said nothing.

"Mr. Doe." The man in the suit waited.

When Jack looked him in the eye again, he continued.

"I assure you this is not the case. You were not at fault, and the bond between you and your brother was never in danger."

Jimmy rose to his feet and placed a hand on Jack's shoulder.

The man went on. "You, of all people, should understand the strength of bonds between loved ones. To think that something as commonplace as death could weaken that bond is the height of foolishness."

A high, sharp beeping noise suddenly resonated from one of the machines near Ms. Dubois. The Doe brothers turned toward her in surprise.

However, as nurses entered the room—as the man in the dark suit subtly faded into the background—they both heard him whisper, "You must never forget that."

$$\Delta$$

In the Hinderwood, Ben smiled—a new activity for him, at least in recent years. The woods rarely made him happy; he was easily frightened, despite his size. Mostly, Ben hated how lonely he felt there.

But he'd found a way to solve that problem. He made a new friend.

His new companion wore jeans, a black-hooded sweatshirt, and glasses he cleaned often, though Ben never saw them get dirty. They met recently when Ben went looking for his other friend, the one with the baseball bat. He noticed the man wore a rifle over his back that looked a lot like Jack's.

The man surprised him by approaching him and asking very frankly, "Can you help me with something?"

Ben replied, "Okay."

Later, after several hours of walking, Ben and his new friend Drew found themselves standing with their backs to a massive, white wall, staring down at a bleak valley filled with carnage. Ben had been nervous about traveling so far, because he wanted to stay close to town in case his brother showed up. But it felt nice to help Jack Doe, even nicer to have a new friend—and strong people were supposed to help others.

Nonetheless, when he saw the scene of devastation, he began to rethink his decision.

The tall man started to tremble, but Drew placed a reassuring hand on his shoulder. He pointed to a tower with a broken window on the far side of valley.

"You're okay. We just need to get to that building," he said.

Ben nodded, and together they marched through the rocky, black ground.

When they arrived at the smattering of headstones and the scattered remains of the twice-dead, Ben whimpered slightly. His friend told him to close his eyes—then, the bespectacled man led him by the hand until they passed the necrotic scene. When he opened his eyes and saw that they stood outside the heavy oak door of the tower, Ben breathed a sigh of relief.

"How strong are you?" asked the man in the black sweatshirt.

"Really strong," said Ben, confidently.

"Well, this door is locked, and we need to get inside."

"I can help."

Ben reached out a hand that could have palmed a pumpkin and placed it on the solid door. He pushed—not hard—more to test the strength of the barricade. Then, he nodded to himself and took a step back.

With a deep breath and a loud grunt, Ben planted a powerful kick in the center of the door. The thud echoed through the empty valley, but the door remained in place.

Bracing himself, he kicked two more times, causing a deep crack to appear on the third impact. With one last breath, Ben lowered his shoulder, roared, and charged forward.

The door broke and the barricade splintered, snapping in on itself like a popsicle stick.

When he rose to a knee amidst the broken wood, breathing heavily, his friend offered him a hand and helped him to his feet. "Good job."

Ben smiled.

Then they walked up a set of stairs so narrow, Ben had to ascend them sideways. Halfway up, they reached a room like a medieval doctor's office.

His friend didn't waste any time—he walked directly toward a tall shelf that held dozens of glass jars filled with red sand. All were sealed tight with crude leather covers and waxed twine.

"Stand back," his friend warned.

Ben stepped back against one of the stone walls.

Drew grabbed the crude, wooden shelf and heaved. When the makeshift cabinet tipped, the jars all slid forward. Then, his friend pushed harder, and they all fell and crashed to the cold stone floor.

Ben winced at the sound of breaking glass, but his eyes widened when the red sand began swirling violently around the room.

As the two men watched, dozens of distinct red lights emerged from the blood-colored dust. Lights continued to appear until the red sand disappeared entirely. The shimmering illuminations circled once more around the room, then filed out the broken window. When the last one disappeared, Ben's new friend nodded and motioned for him to follow him back down the stairs.

When Ben stepped over the wooden debris that used to be a door, he found that he and Drew were no longer alone in the dark valley. Even more surprisingly, all the corpses and rotten scenes of carnage had disappeared.

Dozens of children stood in a tight group outside the tower, staring up at the two adults expectantly. The children's clothing outlined a fashion timeline going back a hundred years. Some wore rough, handspun suits and dresses, while others sported relatively modern jeans and t-shirts. But all the clothes were slightly dusty, and all the children had a slightly sleepy look—as if just waking from a long slumber.

"What're you kids doing here?" asked Ben.

"We've been here a long time," replied a blond girl with big eyes.

Understanding dawned on the towering man.

His friend stepped forward. "Then, it's probably time for us to leave." He started back toward the immense, white wall. "Follow us."

As Ben Morningside and Drew Eldridge led the way out of the valley, the children began to talk amongst themselves. Ben smiled when he heard some of the kids laughing at a joke. Then, the blond girl sang a silly song.

Once they reached the white gate, Drew brightened up, asking the group at large, "Any of you want to learn to play chess?"

Δ

For the first time he could remember, Jack wore a suit: black and formal but plain. He wore a matching necktie, which Cash showed him how to tie correctly. Jimmy, who stood next to him sporting a bandaged hand, wore a smaller but otherwise identical suit.

William Porter gave both suits to the Doe brothers. He wore a similar affair, though he stood far off, away from the crowd of people gathering around the burial plot. His and Ceri's silhouettes watched from a respectful distance.

Jack never expected such a large crowd, but he'd been foolish to think Renee Dubois's funeral would be anything other than a packed house. Ms. Dubois lived a long life and touched many hearts as the town's storyteller, and librarian, and otherwise. She made a significant impact on the town of Opossum Trot, and many turned out to pay their respects.

Buford gave the eulogy, to Jack's surprise. He didn't speak long, but he talked about Ms. Dubois's faith, hope, and seemingly limitless supply of love—often for those who wouldn't find it anywhere else. He struggled to clear his throat as he formed the last words.

Others spoke as well, including the Mayor, the Sheriff, and several other members of the community. One of the last to speak was a man with serious eyes who looked familiar to Jack, though the boy couldn't say how.

The man simply said, "She was a hero." Then, to Jack's surprise, he produced one of Ms. Dubois's home-made dog treats and placed it tenderly on the coffin. That finished, he went to stand beside Mayor Dane and a pretty woman who held a large pit bull on a leash.

After the service, Jack and Jimmy shook a lot of hands, gritting their teeth through many hugs. Once the procession of adults finished, they were both happy to see a more welcome band of mourners approaching.

The Doe brothers hadn't seen Scott, Amelia, or Claire since splitting up on Halloween.

Scott didn't make eye contact, but Amelia and Claire wrapped the Doe brothers in the only hugs of the day that didn't make them wince. Jack caught the familiar scent of Claire's green apple soap, and he felt annoyed when a blush rose up on his cheeks.

Once the displays of affection and support ended, Amelia spoke first. "You two are starting to look like mini morticians," she said, staring at the brother's new black suits.

Claire poked her in the ribs, reprimanding, and asked, "How are things going at his house?"

"It's not so bad," Jimmy said. "He's quiet, but he's okay when you get to know him."

"I know the type." Claire looked at Jack knowingly.

Jack smiled slightly and replied, "The dog's cool."

Suddenly, Scott said, "I'm glad you're okay," without looking up.

"Thanks, Scott," said Jimmy.

Jack said nothing, but he reached into the inner pocket of his suit coat.

When he held his hand out to Scott, the younger boy stared at him with a puzzled expression, but eventually, he held out his hand.

Jack said, "You were right, I could use some more practice." Then, he handed over the black knight chess piece. "It's a good thing I keep running into smart opponents."

Scott said nothing—he just stared fixedly at the black game piece. When he turned it over, his eyes widened at the markings on the bottom.

For the first time, he raised his eyes and met Jack's gaze. "What was on the other side of that door?"

Before Jack could answer, Buford and Cash strolled over.

"You kids clear on off, now. They can catch up with you later," said Cash.

"Yep. We need a word," agreed Buford.

Claire and Amelia shrugged and walked off with Scott, who looked back at Jack curiously.

Once they were out of ear shot, Cash put a hand on Jack's shoulder. "You boys doing alright?"

"Yes, sir," Jimmy replied. Jack shrugged.

"Renee was a good woman. You boys were lucky to know her," said Buford.

"And she thought the world of you," added Cash.

"I think she liked y'all, too," said Jimmy.

"Well, I said she was a good woman, not that she had good taste." Buford smiled wryly.

"Anyways, how things going with the under-taker?" asked Cash.

Jack shrugged again.

"There's something off about that fella. Always thought so," said Buford.

"Don't make sense to me, them sending you boys to live with him," said Cash, thoughtfully.

"We offered," Buford added. "Even asked Hank about it. But he told us it had already been worked out."

"And that we had too many guns lying around," Cash remarked.

"Thanks for looking out," said Jack, sincerely. "But Mr. Porter's alright."

"Well, just 'cause you living there doesn't mean we're going anywhere," said Buford, firmly.

"Yep, you need anything, we'll be around. That's a promise," Cash agreed.

The Doe brothers nodded.

The old men turned to leave, but Buford raised a finger, as if remembering something. He turned back and added, "Oh, and you still owe me for that rifle you lost. So, you need to be at work early on Monday."

$$\Delta$$

At the edge of the cemetery, William Porter and Ceri stood beside a man in a neat, dark suit. They watched the mourners slowly file away until the Doe brothers stood alone beside Ms. Dubois's coffin.

The two men stared in silence, until William Porter finally asked, "So, now I'm a babysitter? Door hasn't opened in over a hundred years. Mess up one time, and now this."

"They are resilient young men who will accomplish much good in the years to come. You have a lot to teach them… and to learn from them."

William Porter seemed unconvinced, but Ceri wagged her tail slightly.

"Are there any other issues I need to be aware of? I don't think anything got through, but the gate was open for a long time."

"You did an admirable job. However, one did escape," the man in the black suit replied, flatly.

William Porter started in surprise. Turning, he looked the man in the eye, though doing so for any period of time made him dizzy. "What? Not one of the ancient ones?"

"No. Much worse."

"Worse? What could be worse?"

"It's not your concern. At least, not for some time. He will likely need to rest for several years. Crossing over requires a lot of energy."

"Who is it?"

"I cannot say." The neat man straightened his glasses slightly. "But it would be wise to prepare yourself, William Porter, and your new charges. You will need all the help you can muster." He looked out over the town, then sighed, "There are strange times ahead."

# EPILOGUE

Renee opened her eyes and frowned. She stood in a dark and—in her opinion—rather dilapidated house. Even with no overhead lighting, she saw that the home had been neglected for some time. A layer of dust covered almost every visible surface, dirt obscured the broken windows, and the wallpaper peeled off the walls. Furthermore, a large oak tree grew right through the center of the room. The layout reminded her of William Porter's house, but without the meticulously-sanitized and -maintained quality of the mortician's home.

She scanned the dark room for a light switch but found none. Walking over to one of the windows, she saw the moon casting a faint glow on a wooded landscape. When she squinted, she noticed several dark shapes skittering through the oaks and their tangled curtains of Spanish moss. She frowned again and stepped backward.

Something creaked upstairs, and she noticed a faint, yellow glow from the stairway.

Renee ascended the creaking wooden steps as the light grew stronger, allowing her to see more clearly. At the top, she found a hallway leading to three rooms.

The light came from under the door of the middle room, so she walked forward and turned the knob.

A boy stood in the room, almost as tall as Jack but thinner. He wore a long, olive coat and dirty hiking boots. On his face, he wore a plastic fox mask, and its painted eyes stared blankly at her.

A lesser person would have been alarmed, but Renee did not rattle easily—and besides, she knew how to see beyond masks.

"Hello, young man," she said, with a soft smile.

The spirit with the fox mask remained silent.

Renee stepped toward him and raised her hands, pleased when he didn't move away. "Let's get a better look at you."

When she reached out for the fox mask, the wearer flinched slightly—but again, he made no move to stop her.

Renee removed the mask delicately, then stepped back to examine the young man.

Upon closer observation, Renee recognized the young man as more of a child—no more than five or six—and the clothes he wore suddenly looked far too big for him. She smiled at his shock of red hair and at the intense, green eyes that reminded her of Jack and Jimmy.

Patting him warmly on the shoulder, Renee looked around. She saw only a few personal items: a bed and a bookshelf, with worn copies of *The Adventures of Huckleberry Finn* and *The Adventures of Tom Sawyer* sitting together. Compared to the rest of the house, the room felt homey. Nonetheless, it would simply not do. She turned back to the boy.

"Are you alone here?" she asked.

"Yes." The boy looked at his feet, and Renee didn't miss the sadness in his answer or the tremble in his voice.

She scanned the dimly lit room again and gazed out the dirty window. "Right. Well, that won't do at all." She leaned down and smiled at the boy. "This doesn't seem like a good place for a child."

As she said so, the room grew brighter, and Renee noticed a new door in one corner of the room. The door stood open, and a warm, golden light emanated from just beyond the threshold.

Renee nodded. She couldn't have articulated why, but she knew it was right. She held out a hand to the lonely child. "I think you'd better come with me."

$$\Delta$$

The red-haired boy took her hand and followed her through the doorway.

As the golden light enveloped them both, he wondered how long it would be before he saw his brothers again. He didn't feel sad, though. When his brothers were ready, they'd find him.

After all, when it came down to death and eternity versus all three Doe brothers, he knew better than anyone.

It was hardly a fair fight.

# ACKNOWLEDGEMENTS

This book represents the efforts of many patient and long-suffering individuals. I would like to thank my editor Julie Elise Landry for her hard work and encouragement as a deeply personal story was shaped into something polished and professional. I would also like to thank Teo Skaffa for the artwork and his continued ability to bring the world of *Jackalope Stories* to life. I am also grateful to the town of Liberty, Mississippi, for making Opossum Trot so easy to visit. Finally, I want to thank my wife and family members who heard every version of this tale before *The Hinderwood* finally emerged.

# About the Author

Jake Nickens was born and raised in Southern Mississippi. He spent his childhood listening to family tall tales and reading comic books that turned him into the kind of adult who writes stories about consecrated baseball bats and wooden sheds leading to the Underworld. He enjoys watching the original *Twilight Zone*, reading comic books, and testing out new takes on Southern cooking. He lives in Louisiana with his wife Lydia and their Akita, Ceri.